Mr. Safe (Jordan)	Mr. Sexy (Charles)
Takes me to Mom's for dinner	Wines and dines me at my favorite restaurants
Gives me a peck on the cheek at the door	Ravishes me with searing kisses that cause my knees to knock
Familiar	Never stops surprising me, enchanting me
Can't lose	Can't win

Would a comfortable relationship be enough...?

Dear Reader,

Thanks so much for your wonderful response to the
HOW TO MARRY... trilogy we brought you earlier
this year. You loved those romances and told us you
wanted more. And we listened!

We're happy to bring you more fun-filled
HOW TO MARRY... books—this time it's
A Reluctant Rogue, by Pam McCutcheon. Like
A Million-Dollar Man, One Hot Cowboy and
The Bad Boy Next Door, this rogue is sexy—and
sure to make your toes curl! You'll delight in how he
teaches our heroine a thing or two about real passion.

Pam McCutcheon lived all over the world in her
career as an industrial engineer for the air force, but
when it came time to write this book, she went back
to her Arizona roots and remembered childhood tales
of the Old West. Now a full-time writer, she lives in
Colorado Springs with her two dogs.

In the months ahead we'll be bringing you some more
HOW TO MARRY... books. Be on the lookout for the
distinctive packaging.

Happy reading!

Regards,

Debra Matteucci
Senior Editor & Editorial Coordinator
Harlequin Books
300 East 42nd Street
New York, NY 10017

HOW TO MARRY...

A RELUCTANT ROGUE

Pam McCutcheon

Harlequin Books

TORONTO • NEW YORK • LONDON
AMSTERDAM • PARIS • SYDNEY • HAMBURG
STOCKHOLM • ATHENS • TOKYO • MILAN
MADRID • WARSAW • BUDAPEST • AUCKLAND

As always, my gratitude to the Wyrd Sisters for keeping me sane; with special thanks to Frank and Mae Boles for sharing the legend of Black Bart and for driving me all over Sedona; to Paula Gill, Carol Umberger and Doreen McKnight for reading and proofing the entire manuscript; and to Linda Kruger, agent extraordinaire, for believing in my screwy ideas.

ISBN 0-373-16696-6

A RELUCTANT ROGUE

Printed in U.S.A.

Chapter One

"My life is ruined," Marigold Boles declared in an angst-ridden voice, then peered at the object of her dramatics to gauge their effect. Maybe it was a bit over the top, but that was what it took to get Kirby's attention.

"Mmm-hmm," he said, without even looking up from his computer.

Okay, so it didn't work. Then again, she really hadn't expected it too. Mari sighed in exasperation and rested her hands on her hips. "Kirby Jones, you are a walking cliché."

A nineties version of the absentminded scientist, her skinny boss rarely wore anything but scruffy jeans, T-shirts and tennis shoes. His disheveled light brown hair was in constant need of a cut and his wire-framed glasses never seemed to stay in place on his nose.

"Kirby," Mari repeated, knowing from long experience that she needed patience and persistence to break through his intense concentration.

"Hmm?"

Well, that was progress anyway. "My life is ruined," she repeated.

"Uh-huh." He continued typing, his glasses sliding inevitably down his nose.

Damn. It was time to pull out the big guns. She took a deep breath, then said, "Kirby, I need you."

It took a moment for the words to penetrate the dense fog of his intellect. He glanced up, shoved his glasses into place and blinked at her. "Why didn't you say so?"

She knew that'd get him. Since they'd met and become friends in third grade, Kirby had never been able to resist that phrase. He loved being needed, and there was no one he enjoyed helping more than Mari. Fearing overuse of the magic words would diminish their power, Mari only used them when she had to.

Kirby pushed away from his computer and wandered out of the garage-turned-laboratory that separated their duplexes into his kitchen. Acting out of long habit, he grabbed a can of cola from the fridge as Mari poured herself a cup of tea and they settled down at the scarred kitchen table.

Kirby took a swig of his drink and favored her with his customary piercing stare. The look intimidated some people, but Mari took it as a compliment that he gave her the same intense concentration he gave his work.

"Okay, what is it?" Kirby asked. "I'll bet it's about your fiancé…" his eyes unfocused for a minute as he tried to force his brain into unaccustomed pathways "…Gordon, right?"

"Jordan. His name is Jordan." Mari was impressed—Kirby rarely remembered anyone's name or even got this close. Maybe he really had been listening.

"Yeah, Jordan. Well, was I right?"

"Yes, it's about Jordan."

Kirby nodded, smiling fatuously. He didn't often recognize or understand anything people related, but when he did he was unbearably smug about it.

Oddly enough, he was modest about his scientific accomplishments—and they were truly impressive. A theoretical scientist who worked for some hotshot think tank in southern California, Kirby had a reputation for combining the unlikeliest things and coming up with inventions no one had even thought of before.

His employers humored him, knowing they'd get value for their money if they just left him alone, which was why he was able to work here in his hometown of Sedona, Arizona. With its artsy New Age culture, it was a strange place for a theoretical scientist to choose to work, but that didn't deter Kirby.

"What's wrong?" he asked.

"Jordan's parents hate me."

Kirby's eyebrows rose. "That's a strong word, hate."

"Yes, but true. They found out about Black Bart."

"Black Bart?"

"Yes, you know how proud my parents are of being descended from Black Bart's brother."

"Oh, yeah. That."

How could anyone forget it? Her parents bragged about being related to Charles Boles, aka Black Bart, at every opportunity. "Well, the Sloans—Jordan's parents—heard about it and threw a snit."

Kirby's brow wrinkled. "I don't get it. Why should they care?"

"It has something to do with the fact that they made all their money by investing in Wells Fargo."

"So?"

"Black Bart made all his money by *stealing* from Wells Fargo—he was an infamous Wild West stage-coach robber, remember?"

"They don't like you because of that?"

She shrugged. "Apparently."

"That's dumb. Your stepfather may have adopted you, but Black Bart's blood runs in *his* veins, not yours."

"I know—but that wouldn't make any difference to the Sloans. To them, family is family, regardless of bloodline. Jordan hinted to them about our engagement, but they refused to listen. Instead, they're going to invite women from all over the state—rich women in his social sphere—to his birthday party this month, in hopes of finding him a suitable wife."

"And you're...not invited?"

Obviously, Kirby still didn't understand her problem. "Oh, I'm invited. Jordan made sure of that."

"So what's wrong?"

"How can I compete with those women? They're rich, beautiful and have pedigrees that go back to the *Mayflower,* for heaven's sake. On the other hand, I'm poor, plain and a total klutz."

"I could give you money."

Mari smiled at her friend. He would, too. "You already pay me far more than any assistant deserves."

"That's not true. Before you agreed to work for me, I couldn't get a decent assistant—they kept quitting on me. You're always here when I need you, which is more than I can say for anyone else."

True, but then how many people would put up with being woken at three o'clock in the morning to help with an experiment or being pulled away from a quiet evening at home to type a report? Mari didn't mind because she knew and loved Kirby. No one else would be so tolerant. "Money isn't the point."

"But you fix up nice, too. When you..." he made vague gestures around his head "...do stuff to your hair and your face, you look real good."

Do stuff? Mari held back a chuckle. Inept as he was, Kirby was a loyal friend and good for her ego. That's why she always discussed her problems with him. He had such a unique slant on things, he usually jolted her thinking onto a different path and made her stop and analyze what was really important.

"Thank you, but my looks aren't the point, either. Let's face it. I'm a misfit. I never fit in at things like that. I get nervous. And when I get nervous, I turn klutzy and do really dumb things."

"No, you don't," he said with staunch loyalty.

"Come on, Kirby. Remember when you took me to the senior prom? I looked like a frump, wearing my mom's old prom dress. I was so embarrassed I tried to hide behind the punch bowl."

"That wasn't so bad—"

"No? How about when I tripped into the punch bowl and dumped it all over both of us? Sprawling on the floor in front of the entire senior class isn't my idea of fun. My mother wasn't too happy, either. Do you have any idea how hard it is to get red punch out of white tulle?"

She'd never forget the humiliation of that moment. As everyone snickered, she'd vowed to find a way to belong so no one would ever laugh at her again.

"That's only once—"

"No, that's just one of many. I was—am—too shy and logical to mesh with all those artsy types. I just don't get them...and they don't get me. I don't fit in."

Kirby patted her arm awkwardly. "You fit in with me."

"Thanks," she said, but it didn't help. Kirby was a misfit, too. That's why they'd been friends so long. She only wished she could shrug it off like he did—being a misfit had never bothered him. In fact, she doubted he was even aware of it. He lived in his own little universe, conversing with quarks and tachyons, and let the mundane world drift by without him.

"So," Kirby said in hesitation, "you're just going to...quit? Give up your fiancé?"

She didn't want to quit, but... "What choices do I have? I don't have the social background to impress the Sloans and what they do know of my background, they despise."

"What about him? Does he really care what his parents think?"

Mari ducked her head. Jordan hadn't been very forthcoming on that subject. "He says he loves me—"

"Says? It sounds like you don't believe it."

"I don't know—it all happened so fast. We met in an office supply store when we both reached for the same toner cartridge."

Kirby nodded as if it were a perfectly normal occurrence. Mari grimaced. That was the problem with the two of them. Who else would see nothing wrong with finding romance over printer parts? "We started talking and one thing led to another, then we found out we were both loners..."

Loners? Lonely was more like it. Everyone in Mari's life seemed to be a cliché. Jordan, the poor little rich kid, Kirby, the absentminded scientist, and even Mari herself, the shy mousy assistant. All misfits. It was a strange thing to base a relationship on, but it was what had drawn her and Jordan together. But... was it enough to last a lifetime?

It had better be, because Mari only planned on marrying once, and Jordan seemed ideal. Not because he was rich, though that didn't hurt, but because he had the right sort of social connections—the kind that would put her securely in the "belonging" category.

No one would be able to laugh at her if she was Jordan Sloan's wife—the daughter-in-law of Reginald Sloan. Of course, she was very fond of Jordan, too, and confident that affection would soon grow into a lasting love.

"He...he wants to stick up for me, but he doesn't want to hurt his parents, either."

"So what are you going to do?"

"What can I do? It's not like we can choose not to be descended from an outlaw."

Kirby got a faraway look in his eyes. "Maybe you can."

"Yeah, right."

"No, really. What if Black Bart wasn't an outlaw?"

"Then we'd be in an alternate universe. C'mon, Kirby, get real. You'd have to change history."

He nodded. "I can do that."

She regarded him incredulously. "You can do that?" From anyone else, she would have thought they were bragging or hallucinating. But if Kirby said it... "How?"

"Time travel."

"Is that feasible?"

"I think so." Kirby's gaze wandered off to another star system again and he muttered, "I'm sure of it."

"How?" she repeated.

"Hmm?"

"Don't space out on me now, Kirby, I need you. How is time travel possible?"

His gaze came back to the here and now. "Vortexes."

Her heart sank. "Vortexes," she repeated. "You mean those energy whatchamacallits the New Agers claim have special powers?"

"Yes—I've been studying them. Believe it or not, they really do exist, though they don't work the way the mystics think." His voice took on an excited tone and he waved his hands in the air to illustrate. "They're controlled by definite physical laws, and I've discovered the energy flow moves in time as well as space."

Mari raised a disbelieving eyebrow.

"No, really. I've figured out a way to tap into them to move into the past or the future."

He started to explain the theory, but Mari held up a hand to stop him. The finer points of physics and other sciences were beyond her, and she wanted to keep it that way. She'd learned only enough to help Kirby in his experiments without blowing anything up.

"You mean you've built a time machine?" she asked incredulously.

"It's not really a time machine, per se. It just takes advantage of the natural capabilities of the vortex. I call it my energy vortex enhancer—EVE for short." He grinned. "Who better to explore back to the dawn of time than EVE?"

"You're serious about this?"

"Yes. This isn't just off the top of my head. I've been studying this for years. When you interrupted me, I was just putting the finishing touches on my theory. I don't see any reason why it shouldn't work."

"So, you're suggesting I go back in time to…persuade Black Bart away from a life of crime?"

"No, that's too dangerous. I'll bring him here, you convince him and then I'll send him back."

Mari shook her head. She couldn't believe she was hearing this. All she'd wanted was a little simple advice. Instead, she got a half-baked time travel theory. Kirby had obviously never learned the KISS principle.

"Let me get this straight," she said. "You want to bring Black Bart to the present?"

"Yes," Kirby said, as if it were the most natural thing in the world.

"And you want me to convince him to give up a life of crime? How? By all accounts, the man was an out-and-out rogue."

"You figure that part out. I'll just get him here. Besides, I've heard your parents talk about him often enough. He wasn't that bad. He never killed anyone. In fact, he was known as the gentleman poet. How bad could he be?"

Mari sighed. "Why couldn't you come up with something simple? Like advice. Or a pat on the shoulder?"

Kirby gave her the patronizing look he usually reserved for accountants and salesmen. "If you think that'll help…"

"No, of course it won't. But…time travel? Don't

you think that's a little far-fetched? Besides, how are you going to locate one man in time?"

He frowned for a minute, then brightened. "No problem. Your parents know everything about him and his history. Just have them pinpoint him for me at one particular place in time and I'll get him here. Remember, you need to find a time before he robs his first stage or it won't do you any good. It'd be best if he's alone, too, so we don't get someone else by mistake. The rest is up to you."

Mari opened her mouth to argue, then closed it. It was futile. When Kirby got an idea in his head like this, there was no talking him out of it.

Besides, it might even work.

THERE'S NO WAY THIS is going to work, Mari thought as she watched Kirby load equipment in his Jeep. It had been three days since he had come up with this wild idea and he'd spent every minute since perfecting some mad scientist-like contraption that he actually thought would reach out and pluck a man through time.

Unbelievable. The thing looked like a jury-rigged engine that someone had constructed of cannibalized parts haphazardly attached to bits and pieces of household appliances—rather like the warped result of a mating between a television and a vacuum cleaner. Did he really expect this...EVE thing to bring a man through time?

But Kirby was her boss and her best friend...her oldest friend. She couldn't let him down by showing her skepticism. Sighing in resignation, she took a seat in the Jeep. As they drove off, she realized there was one consolation at least. It was so late in the day that everyone would probably be gone from the vortexes, finished with summoning up cosmic energies or whatever they did. With any luck, she and Kirby would be all alone with no one to witness their foolishness.

Kirby interrupted her musings. "Do you have the date?"

"Oh, yeah." Mari pulled a piece of paper out of her pocket. "The only time we can pinpoint Black Bart for sure when he's alone is the day he made his first stagecoach robbery—July 26, 1874. He was on top of Funk Hill in Copperopolis, California. Unfortunately, I don't have the exact time, but we think it was early morning—they're pretty sure he spent the night there, waiting for the stage he planned to hold up."

"Close enough."

"But how can you pick him out of time when he's in California and we're in Arizona?"

"No problem. These vortexes are connected by lines of energy to other vortexes all over the world. I'm sure I can find one that comes close enough to Funk Hill to get our man."

Mari rolled her eyes. Kirby was really getting into this. He might be a brilliant theoretical scientist, but right now he sounded more like the New Agers so prevalent in Sedona, talking about crystals, ancient civilizations and psychic experiences. The only difference was, he used scientific terms.

No matter what words he used, though, it all sounded bizarre to Mari. "Kirby, do you really think—"

"Don't worry. It'll work, trust me. The theory is rock solid. I'm no engineer, but anyone could build the necessary machinery, once you understand the theory. The vortex does all the work. The only problem is, I'm not quite sure which vortex to use.''

''Does it matter?''

''Yes, it does. Let me explain.''

Mari gave him a doubtful look.

''Okay, I'll keep it simple and use the mystics' terminology. They say the vortexes at Bell Rock and Airport Mesa are electric, while the one at Courthouse Rock is magnetic. Really, though, it's just another way to describe the time flows. One leads to the past, one to the present.''

''Which is which?''

''Well,'' Kirby said with uncharacteristic doubt, ''I'm not sure, but my calculations seem to support the idea that what they call the electrical energy is associated with the past, while the magnetic energy is associated with the future. Assuming that's correct, we'll try Bell Rock first.''

''Okay, whatever you say.'' Mari sighed and took in the beauty of the Sedona area as they wound their way out of town. Though she'd lived here all her life, she never tired of this vista. The rich red monolithic rocks, striated with the geological history of sixty-five million years, contrasted with fresh green patches of piñon, juniper and cypress trees.

No wonder Sedona was such a mecca for mystics. With its huge red rocks, shaped by erosion into fanciful spires and buttes, it reminded her of a giant's playground, abandoned long ago and strewn with the discarded toys of some immense child.

One of the largest and most photographed ''toys'' was Bell Rock, a massive bell-shaped rock thrusting up from the mesa. They approached it now in the waning brilliance of an Arizona sunset, the oranges and purples providing a suitable backdrop for this glory of nature.

Kirby parked at the side of the road and Mari noted with relief that most of the visitors were packing up to head home. "Where are we going to do this?" she asked.

"On the top—the energy emits from there into the atmosphere."

"You mean we have to climb that thing? How are we going to get your...EVE up there?"

"No problem. It's not that far, and I've got a light. I've rigged a sling to carry EVE on my back."

"You're kidding, right?"

Kirby was busy pulling out straps and hooking them to the strange machine. "No, it'll work. Trust me. C'mon, help me with EVE."

In resignation, Mari helped him load the surprisingly lightweight contraption onto his back and secured it there with a few straps.

Kirby adjusted the headlamp on his hard hat and peered owlishly at her from behind his glasses. He grinned. "I'm ready. Let's go."

Mari followed Kirby up the rock. *Brother—what I do for my friends.* Forty-five minutes later they reached the top, both huffing and puffing. Neither of them was .very athletic, and climbing this thing in the waning light wasn't easy.

Kirby eased EVE off his back and sat down to rest, wiping his brow with his shirtsleeve. Taking a map out of his pocket, he bent to make notations on a sheet of paper while he muttered to himself.

Mari just relaxed and enjoyed the quiet and serenity of her surroundings as Kirby did his thing. Occasionally he asked her a question or had her hold the light, but otherwise she left him alone, knowing he'd call out if he needed her.

Finally he seemed satisfied. He rose and brushed off the seat of his jeans, saying, "Okay, let's do it. I've figured out exactly how far away Black Bart is in space and time, so all I need to do is set the co-ordinates."

Yeah, right. Like this was really going to work.

Kirby turned the machine on and fiddled with a few dials. Mari felt the crackle of energy in the air as the machine hummed ominously. It glowed violet, and Kirby looked even more like a mad scientist as he bent over the thing. His glasses were askew and his hair stuck up all over as the sickly light shaded his skin color to a pale deathly lavender. Mari stifled a giggle. It reminded her of the old B movies she'd watched as a kid.

The thing hummed on as Kirby made frequent adjustments to the dials, but nothing happened. Finally he switched it off and ran a hand through his already disheveled hair. "It's not working."

"Not working?" Mari was disappointed. She hadn't really expected it to, but she'd kind of hoped it would.

Kirby scratched his head in puzzlement. "It should work, but EVE didn't detect any large life-forms in that place and time."

Mari patted Kirby on the arm. "That's okay. Don't worry about it. I'll just find another way to convince Jordan's—"

"No," Kirby said, cutting her off. "I must've used the wrong vortex. After all, even Benjamin Franklin guessed wrong at first about the direction of electrical flow. Let's try Courthouse Rock."

"Kirby—"

"It'll work, Mari. Trust me. It'll work."

"I really don't feel like climbing any more tonight."

"It's okay—you won't have to. The vortex at Courthouse Rock extends for about five hundred yards around the base—we won't need to do any more climbing. C'mon, you gotta try it. You want to marry Gordon, don't you?" he wheedled.

"Jordan," she corrected automatically. Well, it didn't sound too painful, and she knew stubborn Kirby would try it sooner or later anyway. Might as well make it sooner and get it over with.

Besides, Bell Rock and Courthouse Rock were located very near each other, so it wasn't like they were going far out of their way, after all. "Okay, let's try it."

They made their way down and drove the short distance to Courthouse Rock. Once there, they loaded EVE on Kirby's back again and trudged to the base of the monolith.

He found a spot to his liking, clear of vegetation, and set up the machine while Mari sat down on a rock to wait. The night air was a bit nippy, but not too much so. Thank heavens. It was bad enough she had to sit around watching EVE do nothing, without freezing in the process.

Kirby turned on the machine, bathing their surroundings once more in violet light while the air crackled with energy. Mari felt her hair stand on end and she jerked in surprise when Kirby whooped.

She sat up straight. "What is it?"

"I've got something."

Mari moved closer. "You're kidding. What?"

Kirby motioned her behind him. "Stand back out of the way. I've got a life-form."

"What kind of life-form?"

Kirby's small frame nearly vibrated with excitement. "I think it's human." He turned a couple of dials. "Let's find out."

The air warmed perceptibly and the atmosphere sparked with energy. Mari felt the buildup of some kind of force, then watched as a million pinpoints of light twinkled before her. No—it couldn't be. It looked just like the transporter beam on *Star Trek*. As she watched in disbelief, the form of a man emerged and solidified.

"Gotcha," Kirby yelled and switched off the machine.

The man they'd just snatched out of nowhere took one look at them, then his eyes rolled up as he crumpled to the ground.

My God, it worked. It really worked. Stunned, Mari realized Kirby had just brought a man from the past to the present. She stared down at the unconscious form, not believing her eyes. Yes, it was a man. A very real man.

A very naked man.

Chapter Two

"You did it," Mari whispered in awe as she stared down at the unconscious man sprawled facedown on the ground. "You actually brought a man through time."

"I told you I could," Kirby said, a trace of hurt in his voice.

"Yes, I know, but—" Mari broke off. It was useless to explain how far-fetched and extraordinary this event was—how wondrous. For anyone but Kirby, that is. "Do you really think this is Black Bart?"

"If the time and place you gave me are correct, then yes, this is him."

Of course. Kirby rarely made mistakes with anything scientific. Interpersonal relationships, on the other hand... "He isn't waking up. Do you think he's okay?"

Kirby knelt next to the man and felt his pulse. "He's alive. He's probably just in shock. But it won't do him any good to leave him lying here. C'mon, help me get him up and into the Jeep."

Kirby was right. Now that the machine had shut off, the air was turning cool again. It wouldn't do to give her great-great-great-granduncle pneumonia before she convinced him to give up his life of crime.

Kirby turned him over and Mari felt her cheeks warm. She'd seen naked men before, but not very many and certainly none who looked like this.

He appeared to be about five feet ten inches tall, built nicely lean, with just enough muscles on him to make him look all man. The strong planes of his face were framed by shaggy dark hair and his wide chest, furred with the same dark hair, narrowed to a trim waist. Below that she didn't dare let her gaze wander—she was flushed enough as it was.

Kirby picked up Black Bart's shoulders and said, "C'mon, Mari, grab his feet."

Mari did as he asked and somehow managed to help Kirby carry the unconscious man to the Jeep without letting her gaze stray where it shouldn't. Kirby settled the man in the back seat, then packed up his equipment and stowed it in the rear. Mari watched their passenger anxiously, but Black Bart stayed unconscious for the remainder of the trip.

When they reached the duplex, she realized it might look a little odd if her neighbors were to see them carrying a naked man into the house, so she ran inside to grab a blanket. She wrapped it around him, then helped Kirby lift him out of the Jeep.

They paused for a moment to secure their grip, then Mari stepped toward Kirby's door at the same time he moved toward hers. Black Bart folded in the middle between them.

"What are you doing?" she asked in a whisper, trying not to disturb the neighbors.

"Taking him into your house."

"Yes, but...he's a man."

"I can see that," Kirby whispered back. "So?"

"I can't have a strange man staying with me. What will people say?"

"Nothing. He's your relative, isn't he?"

She gave their burden a dubious glance. "Yes, but...it's gonna be awfully hard to explain how we're related."

"Just tell people you're cousins."

It made sense, but... "Can't you just keep him at your house?"

"You know I hate having guests. Besides, I met my end of the bargain. I got him here—the rest is up to you."

Mari frowned in indecision as she stared down at the man who it now seemed would be her houseguest. "But...what if he's dangerous?"

"History says he's not."

"Yes, but we've just brought him to another time and place where he's bound to be confused and upset. Anyone would be angry in that situation. What if he gets...violent?"

Kirby sighed. "Oh, all right. I'll stay with you until he wakes up, okay?"

That wouldn't be much help—the guy had to outweigh Kirby by at least forty pounds. But it would be two against one, and they had the advantages of being on home ground and understanding this technological society while he didn't. It would have to do.

Besides, they couldn't stand here arguing all night over his limp body. "All right, let's put him in my guest room, then."

They put him in bed under the covers. He seemed fine except for being unconscious, so they decided not to take him to the hospital. It would be difficult enough to explain what had happened to him, without the added complication of trying to justify why there was no record of his existence.

She could see it now. "Well, Doc, we figure he was blindsided by wild tachyons when we brought him through time with our handy, dandy vortex enhancer." Yeah, right.

As she stared at the unconscious man now resting in her guest room, Mari marveled at how ordinary it all seemed. This was Black Bart, for heaven's sake.

Well, actually he wasn't Black Bart yet. His real name was Charles Boles. She'd just call him Charles. Not Uncle Charles—he certainly didn't look like anyone's great-great-great-granduncle.

Or was it Charlie? She glanced down at his face again. No, Charlie didn't fit the image of a gentleman stagecoach robber. She'd call him Charles.

And when he woke up, she was going to have to convince Charles to give up a life of crime. How in the world was she supposed to do that? The man was supposedly intelligent and well-educated so he wouldn't fall for just anything. Hell, she couldn't convince a salesclerk to give her the time of day—how was she going to persuade this rogue to change his ways?

That question occupied her over the coming hours, as she and Kirby took turns watching him. It certainly wasn't a hardship. She'd seen men like Charles on television and in the movies, but never this up close and personal. Even in his unconscious state, he exuded virility and a primitive vital presence that dominated the small space.

She gazed at his strong, masculine face, wondering idly what color his eyes were, then let her gaze wander lower to the dark swirls of hair on his chest. What would it be like to touch that hard chest, to stroke her fingers through the soft-looking hair?

She reached toward him, but he moved slightly and she jerked her hand back. What was she thinking? This man could be dangerous. Sitting on her wayward hands, she continued her vigil until he stirred again at about seven the next morning.

She shook Kirby's shoulder to wake him from his makeshift bed on the floor. "He's coming to," she whispered fiercely.

Kirby blinked, then put on his glasses and peered at the man in the bed. They both watched avidly as Charles opened bleary eyes and gazed at them.

Blue, Mari thought irreverently. *His eyes are bright blue.*

He groaned, then laid his head back down on the pillow and rubbed his forehead. "Who are you?"

"I'm your...niece."

"My niece?"

"Yeah, sort of. I'm Mari. And this is my friend Kirby."

He frowned at them. "Where am I?"

His penetrating blue gaze made her heart skip a beat. "In my house." She was deliberately vague, knowing it would take a while for him to adjust to the strangeness of all this.

He glanced around the room with a puzzled expression, then shuttered it, his face turning impassive. He was probably confused by the strange surroundings—they weren't exactly familiar trappings for someone from 1874. But thank heavens he didn't seem to be upset...yet.

"How about you?" she asked tentatively. "Do you prefer to be called Charles or Charlie?"

His brow wrinkled as he stared at her in puzzlement. "Char—?" He shook his head. "It doesn't matter. Call me what you like." He sounded totally indifferent.

"Okay. Charles, then." Mari fell silent, not knowing what else to say.

"How do you feel?" Kirby asked.

"My head hurts," he admitted. "What happened?"

Mari and Kirby exchanged glances. Mari shrugged, not knowing how to break it to him gently. Let Kirby figure that out.

"Well," Kirby said, "it's like this. We brought you through time to 1997."

Mari elbowed Kirby in the ribs. "Gee, great job of breaking it to him easy," she muttered.

Kirby just shrugged and they both looked expectantly at Charles.

"The past?"

"Yes, we brought you from the past," she confirmed.

"Through time," he repeated flatly. "I'm in the future?"

"Yeah, pretty much," Kirby said in an offhand manner. "Do you have any questions?"

Charles scowled. "How'd I get here?"

"We brought you," Kirby admitted with the air of a man who didn't know how to lie—or didn't need to.

"Why?" Charles demanded.

Kirby glanced at Mari, obviously tossing the conversational ball into her court. This wasn't the way she wanted to explain it to Charles, but she guessed there really wasn't a good way to do it anyway. Taking her cue from Kirby she told the bald truth, explaining about Jordan and his family's problem with Black Bart.

"You think I am Black Bart, this...this stagecoach robber?" Charles asked.

He seemed to be taking it well enough, but Mari was still a little apprehensive. "Yes. Well, not yet," Mari assured him. "But you're going to be, unless I can convince you otherwise."

"Can you?"

"I don't know, but I'm sure gonna try. My future depends on it."

"Future," Charles mused, as if testing the word on his tongue. "How do you know I am going to be Black Bart?"

"Well, history tells us that Charles Boles, aka Charles Bolton, was Black Bart."

"And how do you know I am Charles Boles?"

Mari regarded him in bewilderment. Had they grabbed the wrong man? "Aren't you...Charles Boles?"

His face turned bleak. "I don't know. I can't remember. I can't remember anything."

HE TESTED THE NAME in his mind. It didn't feel right, but neither did anything else. There was nothing but a big void where his identity should be. So perhaps he *was* Charles Boles. For now, it was something to call himself anyway.

Some of the rest of what they'd said penetrated the fog surrounding his mind. Time travel. The future. He eyed them warily. Was he really in the future...or some home for the criminally insane? The latter seemed entirely possible, since neither one of these inmates made any sense. They looked normal, though.

The man—Kirby—was a type Charles recognized. Small and slight, he appeared single-minded, intent only on one thing. Right now, that thing happened to be Charles.

And the woman...she had possibilities. Slightly taller than her friend, she had an open face with a generous mouth and a turned-up nose. Her thick brown hair fell straight to her shoulders and she peered at him with big brown eyes from under long bangs.

Unfortunately he couldn't tell anything about her figure. She stood hunched over, her arms crossed over her chest, wearing a shapeless sweater over baggy pants and shirt—very odd clothing.

Odd clothing? Now, where had that thought come from? He looked down at his, and found he wasn't wearing any. "Where are my clothes?"

The man—Kirby—said, "I have a theory about that. The machine was designed specifically to retrieve animate beings, so it probably filtered out your clothing because of its inanimate structure."

Charles looked at the woman, his supposed niece, for clarification. "What did he say?"

Mari grinned. "Uh, the vortex ate them?"

Kirby slanted her an annoyed glance. "I figure they're lost somewhere in the space-time continuum or were left behind in the past."

"I see," Charles said doubtfully. He really didn't care what had happened to his clothes. Since he couldn't even remember what he'd been wearing, he hadn't exactly formed a sentimental attachment to them. "Do you think I could impose on you for something to wear?"

"Uh, sure," Kirby replied. He scrutinized Charles as if measuring his size mentally, then left the room muttering.

Mari wrapped her arms awkwardly around her middle. "Look, I know it's hard to believe, but—"

"Wait." Charles held a hand up for silence. "Let me think this through for a moment."

Mari shifted from foot to foot as he perused the room. The lights, the windows, the door, the furnishings—all seemed slightly...wrong. He attempted to discern why they were different, but that was missing, too—gone with the rest of his memory. He might not remember how they were supposed to look, but he did know this wasn't it. It was as if he'd landed in a foreign country or on another planet or...in another time?

Was it possible? He glanced at Mari. She was still watching him with an apprehensive expression. "What year did you say this was?"

"1997."

"And what year did I come from?"

"1874."

He tested the year in his mind. It struck a chord of recognition, and he could almost feel the language of the time period settle in his mind. Perhaps he really had been snatched out of his own time and brought here—1874 certainly felt more familiar than 1997.

Kirby came back in the room and dropped some clothes on the bed. "Uh, I don't have much that'll fit a guy your size, but try these on."

Charles started to pull down the covers, then glanced at Mari.

She reddened. "I'll just..." She gestured awkwardly, then turned around to allow him some privacy.

Charles held up the gray pants, giving Kirby a questioning look.

"It's a sweat suit," Kirby explained. "Just pull the shirt on over your head and pull the pants on the normal way. I didn't bring you any underwear, since I figured mine would be too small to be comfortable, but I did bring you some socks."

The little man babbled on about the clothing, then gazed at Charles with a hopeful expression. Charles paused in puzzlement. What did he expect?

"Uh, thanks," Charles said.

That seemed to satisfy Kirby, and he watched as Charles pulled on the unfamiliar garments. They were easy enough to put on but were a little tight, molding themselves to his body like a second skin. The pants rode a little high on his legs and the sleeves missed his wrists by a good six inches. He fixed the sleeves by pushing them up, and pulled the white socks up to the tight band at the bottom of the pants.

There. He probably looked ridiculous, but at least he was dressed and didn't feel quite so vulnerable. And if the pants weren't quite so tight in the crotch he might even feel comfortable.

Kirby glanced at Mari, saying, "You can turn around now."

She did so, and froze when she saw Charles. Her gaze raked his body, then she colored again and looked away. "We'll get you some decent clothes later."

"Decent?" Kirby repeated. "These are decent."

"Maybe, but they're a little...snug, don't you

think? You did your best, Kirby, but we don't want him to stick out like...never mind.''

Kirby frowned. "He looks okay to me. Besides, we can get him some more clothes later."

Charles was getting a little impatient with them talking about him as if he weren't there. Thirsty, too. "Excuse me?" They both turned to look at him. "May I have some water?"

"Sure," Mari said. She gestured toward the door. "Why don't we all go to the kitchen?"

Wanting to take some sort of control of this impossible situation, Charles decided to lead the way. He headed for the door and smacked face first into it. Stepping back, he stared at it in puzzlement. Shouldn't it have opened?

Mari stepped forward and pulled the door inward. "It's not a swinging door like you're used to," she explained. "You have to use the knob."

She was being kind, though perhaps a little condescending. She obviously thought he was still woozy. Well, he was. Anyone knew how to open a door. Why had he forgotten such a simple thing?

Charles walked through the doorway and followed Mari down the hall. At least he could still remember how to walk and talk.

The memory loss bothered him, but what really annoyed him was that he didn't know who he was. Not just the mundane things like his name and profession, but what sort of man was he? A lover or a killer? An upright, moral man or a hedonist? He didn't know, and it left him feeling uneasy, rootless.

Mari gestured him into a room he recognized as a kitchen, but again everything appeared slightly off-kilter. He sat on an odd-looking chair and waited while Mari poured him a glass of water. The strange surroundings and clothing, coupled with the unusual words and phrases his hosts used, made Charles admit it was quite possible he was out of his own time. And oddly enough that thought didn't shock him as much as it should have.

Mari handed him the glass and he took it, noticing her hand was trembling.

He glanced up and caught an apprehensive expression on her face. "Are you *afraid* of me?"

"No, no. Not really."

Stunned, Charles asked, "How bad was Black Bart, anyway?"

"Not that bad," Mari assured him. "You…he… you *will* be a stagecoach robber, but you never shot anybody."

That was a relief, but he wasn't sure he liked the idea of being a thief. It didn't seem to fit with what he thought of himself, either. Nothing did, but then, according to them he hadn't become Black Bart yet, anyway. "So if I am 'not that bad,' why are you so frightened?"

Mari shrugged and wrapped her arms around her body. "You may have been known as the gentleman poet, but you were still a rogue."

A rogue…now there was a word that resonated within him. He rather enjoyed the idea of being a rogue. Charles paused to let the idea settle into his being. He smiled. It was comforting to have a more definite idea of a personality he could call his own. It helped anchor him, gave him more substance.

Mari looked wary and Charles smiled more broadly, putting some effort into it, becoming more comfortable with the role. He caught her hand and squeezed it. Letting his voice drop to a caress, he said, "Don't worry, I would never hurt you."

Mari blushed and tugged her hand away, almost knocking his glass over in the process.

"That's what I told her," Kirby said, sounding smug. "After all, she's your great-great-great-grandniece."

"Like that's a real close relationship," Mari mocked, rolling her eyes and giving Kirby a friendly little shove.

Charles watched the byplay with interest. With him, Mari was shy and awkward, but around her friend she became confident and playful. He rather liked this side of her and wished she'd treat him the same way. Perhaps she would—if he could get her to trust him.

Kirby rose. "Well, now that *that's* settled, I'll just get back to work—maybe I can find some information on how to treat amnesia."

"Wait," Mari protested.

She drew Kirby over to the side, where Charles couldn't hear what they were saying. They muttered for a while, then Kirby left and Mari came back to sit at the table, eyeing him warily.

"Really," Charles said with a grin, "I won't bite."

"Be sure you don't," Mari said in a challenging tone.

Charles chuckled. Being a rogue was rather amusing—no wonder he'd become one. But...he'd also become a thief, an outlaw. How could he reconcile that with the sort of person he felt he should be? It just didn't fit. Or perhaps he didn't want it to fit?

Turning serious, he gazed down at the glass cradled

in his hands. "Tell me again why you brought me here?"

"I need to reform you," Mari explained. "To convince you not to rob Wells Fargo, so Jordan's parents won't turn up their noses at me."

He raised a quizzical eyebrow at her. "Don't you think your methods were perhaps a little...drastic?"

Mari chuckled. "Yes, as a matter of fact, I do. It was Kirby's idea. All I wanted was a little advice. Instead, he gave me...you."

"And what precisely are your plans for me?"

Mari's gaze slid away from his. "I'm not sure—"

A chime sounded throughout the house, startling him and breaking off whatever she'd been about to say.

Mari gestured in the direction of the sound. "That's a doorbell. Someone's here. Uh, just wait here. I'll be right back."

She hurried away and Charles heard the door open. A man's voice said, "Hello, dear."

"Jordan, what a...nice surprise. What are you doing here?"

Jordan? Curious, Charles looked out the kitchen doorway, where he had a good view of Mari and her fiancé as she gestured him inside and shut the door.

Slender and unprepossessing, Jordan wore all white—white shoes, socks, short pants and shirt. His face was pale, topped by thinning blond hair worn short and under its owner's precise control. In fact, control seemed to be the watchword for this stiff, unsmiling man. Charles grimaced. This was the man Mari loved?

"We had a date to play tennis, remember?" Jordan

scanned her, his lips pursed in disapproval. "You're not dressed for it."

Mari put a hand to her mouth. "Oh, I forgot. I'm so sorry."

Jordan scowled. Feeling partially responsible for the situation, Charles stepped out into the hallway. "I'm afraid that's my fault," he said.

Jordan's eyes narrowed. "Who's this?"

Charles stuck out his hand. "I'm Mari's..."

"Cousin," Mari supplied. "This is my cousin, Charles Boles. Charles, this is my fiancé, Jordan Sloan."

The men shook hands and Charles could feel Jordan sizing him up. Well, he wondered in amusement, had he passed or failed? He couldn't summon much enthusiasm to know the answer.

"Sorry," Charles said, "I arrived late last night. Mari wasn't expecting me. I guess I flustered her so much, she just forgot."

Mari threw him a grateful look, but the scowl hadn't left Jordan's face. "Cousin?" he repeated doubtfully.

"Yes," Mari explained. "On my, uh, father's side. He's, um, Uncle Bertie's son."

"I see," Jordan said in a forbidding tone. Then to Charles, "How long are you going to be here?"

"Jordan," Mari protested in obvious embarrassment.

Charles shrugged. "I'm not sure. That depends on Mari...and Kirby."

"*Why* are you here?" Jordan persisted.

Charles would like to hear the answer to that, himself.

Mari darted him an uncertain glance, then said,

"He's one of Kirby's experi— I mean, he's helping Kirby with an experiment."

"I thought that was your job," Jordan said.

"It is, it is, but this one takes two people and Charles has...expertise I don't that Kirby needs."

"Like what?"

"Does it matter?" Charles interjected before Mari supplied him with some skill he didn't possess.

"I suppose not," Jordan conceded, then raked Charles with his cold gaze. "He isn't staying here, is he?"

"Of course he is. You know how Kirby hates having guests around."

"But what will people think? You already practically live with one man, now two?"

"I thought you understood about Kirby," Mari said in a perplexed tone of voice.

"I do. But Kirby is so...sexless, he's really not a threat." Jordan stared pointedly at Charles in his tight clothing. "I don't think anyone would say that about Charles here."

"I realize that," Mari said and blushed.

Charles grinned. She'd noticed, had she?

"But Charles is my cousin. How can people object to that?"

"Come on, Mari, I'm not stupid. He's from your *step*father's side of the family. There's no blood tie."

"People will know that only if you tell them," Mari answered stubbornly. "I'll just explain to everyone that he's a relative. They don't have to know it's not by blood."

Jordan looked up at the ceiling for a moment, then returned his attention to Mari. "Look, dear, if he wasn't staying here, you wouldn't have to explain."

"What am I supposed to do? Kick him out?"

"No, I'm not saying that, but can't you find somewhere else for him to stay?"

"Where? In a motel? Your house?"

Charles frowned as they discussed his fate. He couldn't allow them to shuffle him off somewhere else. All he wanted was to remain long enough to regain his memory and return to his old life, wherever and whenever that was. When he departed, she could moon over this insipid creature all she wanted. "I don't think that's such a good idea," he said.

Both Jordan and Mari looked at him expectantly. He elaborated, saying, "Until this...experiment is over, I need to stay very close to Kirby and his machine. Don't you agree, Cousin?"

Mari nodded. "He's right, Jordan. Don't ask me to do this. I can't."

Jordan looked distinctly annoyed. "All right, but I don't know what my parents are going to think."

"Then don't tell them," Charles suggested.

"That's right," Mari said. "You don't have to tell your parents everything, do you? In fact," she said in a more belligerent tone, "if you hadn't told them about Black Bart in the first place, I wouldn't be in this mess."

"What mess?" Jordan asked, looking confused.

"Never mind," Charles said, and took Jordan's arm. "She's just tired since I kept her awake all night catching up on the family. I don't think she's in any condition for your date, do you?" As he spoke, he led Jordan to the door and opened it.

Jordan glanced back over his shoulder at Mari and scowled. "But—"

"She's exhausted. If she doesn't get some rest

soon, she might become ill. You wouldn't want that, would you?''

"No," Jordan said hesitantly. "But—"

"Good," Charles said and thrust him out the door. "We'll see you later then. Goodbye."

He shut the door with a satisfying thud in Jordan's face, then turned to see Mari's expression. Amusement warred with indignation on her face. "Thanks," she said. "I think."

"You're welcome." Then, because he had to know, he blurted out, "You brought me through time so you could marry that?"

Chapter Three

Mari's amusement fled. How dare he question her? He knew nothing about her—or her relationship with Jordan. She raised her chin. "Yes, I'm going to marry him. What's wrong with that?"

"He's so stiff...pompous, even. Why would you want to marry such a man?"

Mari turned to walk back to the kitchen, saying over her shoulder, "That's none of your business."

Charles followed her. Though he didn't say anything, she could feel his gaze boring into her back as she took her time pouring tea and adding sweetener. She stood there, stirring it, wishing he would just go away or drop the subject.

"That's not going to help, you know," Charles said.

She turned around and found him leaning nonchalantly against the counter, his arms crossed and a half smile playing around his mouth, looking sexy as hell in his tight sweats.

Heat flashed into her face. Damn. No man should look that good.

She dragged her gaze back up to his face. "It works with Kirby."

"But it won't work with me." He cocked his head to regard her seriously. "You're wrong, you know. It is my business."

Mari leaned on the opposite counter and wrapped her hands around the cup. "How's that?"

"You brought me through time so you could change me. Reform me, you said, so you can marry Jordan. Isn't that correct?"

Mari nodded reluctantly.

"I think I have the right to know why. If I'm to change my…" he gestured with a vague motion, as if looking for just the right words "…nefarious ways, I need a reason."

Irritation coursed through her and she grabbed onto the emotion as if it were a lifeline. "Can't you just change because it's the right thing to do? You were a stagecoach robber, for heaven's sake—a thief. And not a very good one, either. You were caught."

He smiled, laughter twinkling just below the surface in his beautiful blue eyes. "So tell me how I was captured and I'll avoid it."

She couldn't let this rogue charm her into anything. "I can't do that."

"Why not?"

"That's called aiding and abetting. I'd be as guilty as you."

Charles chuckled. "Ah, but you'll have the perfect alibi—when I commit the robbery, you won't even have been born."

He had a point, though she knew he was just teasing her. "Except—"

"That's not the problem, though, is it? You're avoiding the question."

"What question?"

''Why would you want to marry such a man, anyway?''

Her chin rose once more. ''Why not? What's wrong with him?''

Charles quirked an eyebrow at her. ''Well, he isn't very manly, is he?''

Mari could see why he would think that. Jordan probably looked rather odd in his tennis outfit... effeminate, even. Charles, on the other hand, was obviously all man—even wearing a sweat suit. She glanced at him again and revised her opinion. Make that *especially* wearing a sweat suit.

''Maybe not by your standards,'' she conceded, ''but Jordan has other qualities I admire.''

''Such as?''

Mari regarded him in exasperation. She really didn't like talking about her personal life, especially to a stranger. Then again, Charles wasn't a total stranger. He was her uncle. Sort of. ''He's kind and gentle—''

''So's a dog.''

Ignoring that crack, Mari sought for something Charles could comprehend. ''He's intelligent and... and...respected...''

Charles's eyebrows rose. ''What do you mean, respected?''

''His family is highly regarded in this area and they're very well-off.''

''Oh, I see. He's wealthy. Is that why you want to marry him?''

Mari glared at him. ''Don't impose your beliefs on me. I'm not marrying him for his money.''

''No? Then why are you marrying him?''

''Because he understands me,'' she snapped. ''No

one else has ever taken the time or trouble to know the real me.''

Charles's eyes widened. ''I find that hard to believe. Are men so blind in this time that they cannot see your inner beauty?''

Mari shrugged. He sounded just like her father...or an uncle. They were the blind ones, and she wasn't about to let this rogue work his wiles on her. ''Inner beauty doesn't count for much if the outer shell doesn't attract them first. Jordan is the only one who's ever taken the time or trouble to get close enough to learn what I'm really like.''

''I thought Kirby understood you.''

''Well, he does. But Kirby is...Kirby. He's my best friend, not a lover.''

''Is that what you want?'' Charles asked in a low, sexy voice. ''A lover?''

Mari felt her face grow warm. *Yes!* ''Well, naturally, every woman—''

''Then it seems you could do better than Jordan.''

''No, I can't. No one else wants me.'' She wasn't whining or complaining, just stating the plain truth. ''Jordan is special. He's a misfit, too, so he knows exactly how I feel. He understands me...and he loves me.''

''But do you love him?''

Mari averted her gaze. She couldn't lie about something so important, not even to save face. ''I'm very fond of him. I—I'm sure I'll grow to love him.''

The expression on Charles's face was pitying. ''And you would settle for that?''

''Settle? What do you mean, settle? Men aren't exactly lining up to take me out, you know. He's the best chance I've got to finally find a place where I can belong."

Charles stared at her thoughtfully. "Belonging is that important to you?"

"Yes, it's everything, damn it. I've always been on the outside, looking in. I want to be on the inside for a change. I want to be surrounded by a family that loves me as much as I love them—to have friends who care about me, people who don't dismiss me the moment they look at me."

"What about your parents?"

She waved dismissively. "They're too wrapped up in each other to bother with me. Oh, they don't mean to ignore me, and I know they love me, but I don't fit in with them or *their* friends, either. I've never belonged." She wound down as she felt her eyes sting with unshed tears. "Yes, belonging is important."

"And you would give up love to get it?"

She slammed her cup down on the counter. "What the hell do you know about love? You abandoned a wife and four children. Don't talk to me of love."

His face filled with shock and she felt immediate remorse. "Oh, Charles, I'm so sorry. I should've never said that."

Charles sank back against the counter, trying to take in her words. He had deserted a family? What kind of cad was he, anyway?

Once again, he probed his mind, searching for the holes that would be left by a missing wife and children. Still nothing. But that didn't mean anything— his memory was nothing but one large hole.

He gazed at Mari, unsurprised to see contrition and a touch of pity on her face. He didn't want her pity. And perhaps...perhaps he didn't need it. She had to be mistaken. "That doesn't feel right. It doesn't feel like *me*. Are you sure you have the right person?"

Mari nodded. "Kirby never makes mistakes in his experiments—he used the exact date and place my parents gave him. And they know everything about you—they're so proud to be related to you."

"Proud? Proud to be related to a thief and a cad?"

"Yes, it's their only claim to fame, you see. You're the only one in our family tree who ever made anything of himself—good or bad. I think they feel proud they have someone in the history books they can point to and say, 'I'm related to him.'"

Charles found the idea rather sad. Regardless of how much he disliked the idea, he feared he really was a cad and a thief. Unless... "Perhaps I hadn't left my family yet, at the time you took me?"

Mari shook her head. "I'm afraid not. You abandoned your family somewhere in the Midwest, though I don't remember when. But it had to be before we picked you up in California."

"Are you saying you aren't certain of your facts?"

"I'm not—but my parents are."

"Could you ask them, then? To make certain?"

"Not right now—they're out of state, traveling. They won't be back until tomorrow."

Charles didn't know what could have prompted him to desert a family or take to robbery, but it must have been pretty drastic. His memories might be missing but his ethical system was still very much intact, and the current Charles Boles was appalled. "I—I just can't imagine having done that."

Mari brightened. "Then it'll be easier to reform you than I thought."

"Perhaps. But if my memory comes back, then I

might feel different. I might not want to be re-formed."

"We'll just have to hope your memory doesn't come back, then." Mari covered her mouth with her hand. "Oh, I'm sorry. There I go, shooting off my mouth again. Of course you want to get your memory back. I know I would, if I were in your shoes."

"In this instance, I'm not certain I do, but I'll be no use to you if I don't."

"What do you mean?"

"It would be easy to reform me now, when I don't remember anything." And when he felt so eager to please her. But what would happen if he regained Black Bart's memories? "But since the...vortex is what made me lose my memory in the first place, what will happen if you send me back in time again?"

"I see what you mean. You'd probably lose your memory of *this* time...including your reformation." Her expression turned bleak. "What are we going to do?"

"Well, if I could just remember my former life..."

Her face brightened. "Then I could reform you, and when we send you back you'll be more likely to remember it again."

"True. If I can regain my memory now, then chances are good that I can regain it again after you send me back in time."

She nodded slowly. "That makes sense. Okay, let's get started."

"How?"

"I'm not sure. Maybe by learning as much about your former life and time as possible?"

"That appears to be a sound plan. Where shall we start?"

"The library." She gave him a speculative look. "But first, we have to find you some decent clothes. You can't go around town looking like that."

Finally they agreed on something—he definitely wanted to get out of these clothes. At least their argument had one side benefit. She seemed to have lost her fear of him and stopped blushing every time she looked below his neck. She was treating him more like Kirby now, and Charles rather liked it. "But I haven't any way to pay for them."

Mari grinned: "Don't worry about that. Kirby brought you through time and he'll pay for it. It's the least he can do."

"But—"

"It's okay. He has oodles of money and he never spends it on anything. He'll be glad to pay for your clothes, and it won't make even a small dent in his bank account. Besides, he's given me leave until we get you situated. I have lots of time. Let's go."

She grabbed her purse and Charles started to follow her out the door. "Wait. I haven't any shoes."

Mari glanced down at his feet and sighed. "Well, there's no way Kirby's shoes will fit you. We'll just have to buy you some right away. At least your feet are covered." She shook her head as she led the way out the door. "You're going to need everything."

Charles followed her to a large metal contraption outside the house and stood behind her, waiting.

She glanced back, smiling. "You have to get in on the other side."

"Get in? To this?"

"Yes." Mari gestured him around to the other side. "We don't use horses as transportation anymore, we use cars."

Charles went around to the other side and stared down at the car, trying to figure out how to enter it. Shrugging, he said, "Open."

Mari chuckled. "We're not *that* advanced yet. Wait—I'll get it."

She entered the vehicle, then leaned over to open his door. Charles seated himself rather gingerly, then shut his door when he saw Mari close hers. He felt a little hemmed in, even more so when Mari leaned across him to fasten a strap across his chest and waist. "What's that for?"

"It's a seat belt. So you won't get hurt in case we have an accident."

Alarmed, Charles asked, "Is that likely?"

"No, but it's better to be safe than sorry, right?"

"Uh, certainly. Of course." He wasn't convinced.

Mari patted him on the knee. "Don't worry about it. Everything will be fine."

She started the car with a roar and pulled out into the street. As Mari drove through the streets of the small town, Charles goggled at everything he saw. If he wasn't already convinced he'd been transported to another time, this would have accomplished it.

Nothing appeared familiar. Or rather, everything appeared *almost* familiar, as if he ought to recognize things, but they were just different enough that he couldn't determine their functions until Mari explained them to him—like lampposts or water faucets. Then there were items totally beyond his comprehension, like automatic teller machines or traffic signals.

Traffic signals…what an amazing concept. They were nothing more than colored lights that indicated when it was legal to move or not move, yet everyone obeyed them, even when no other people or cars were around. It boggled the mind.

Though the sights filled him with awe, he loathed the feeling of uncertainty they generated in him. Another character trait solidified in his being as he realized being in control was important to him. Unfortunately control was one thing he lacked in this strange world and he made a mental note to right that condition as soon as possible.

Mari stopped in front of a large building and turned off the car. "Well, here we are."

"Where?"

"This is a mall. It has different stores that sell a variety of things, including men's clothing."

Now this was a concept he could understand.

Mari showed him how to unlock his seat belt and exit from the car. They entered the store and here, again, things appeared vaguely familiar, yet somehow wrong, as they wandered through racks and racks of clothes.

Charles looked around in bewilderment. Everything appeared so strange, he couldn't even figure out where to start. He glanced at Mari, but could see she'd be of little assistance. A man approached them and she averted her gaze, wrapping her arms around her middle again, seeming to shrink in on herself.

The man's gaze skimmed right past her as if she didn't exist and settled on Charles with an air of distaste. "May I help you?" he asked in a tone that indicated Charles was beyond assistance.

Charles glanced at Mari again, but she didn't speak. In fact, she seemed so nervous at the thought of talking to a stranger that she backed into a rack, almost knocking it over.

Charles glared at the man who made Mari uncomfortable, then realized he must be a salesman. He even wore a small square with the word "Brad" printed on it. Charles didn't know if that was a piece of hardware or the man's name, but he took a chance on the latter. "Well, Brad, I need clothes."

Brad favored him with a tight smile. "I see. I'm sorry, but we don't carry sweats."

Mari looked mortified, but it only served to make Charles angry. "That's good, because we're not looking for sweats, are we, Mari?"

Mari just shook her head. When he glared at her meaningfully, comprehension dawned on her face and she said, "Uh, right. We're looking for a sports jacket, slacks and some casual clothes—jeans, shirts, underwear, shoes, the works."

Brad glanced aside at Charles, who felt compelled to explain. "I lost all my clothing in…a fire. There's nothing left but this," he gestured down at himself, feeling absurd without shoes, "and it doesn't fit well."

"And what price range were you looking at?"

At a loss, Charles turned to Mari. She dug in her purse and pulled out a small silver card and showed it to Brad. "Price doesn't matter," she said, seeming to gain more confidence. "We just want to find clothes that fit. And fast, so we can get out of here as soon as possible."

Brad's eyes widened as he glanced down at the card. His attitude changed instantly. "Yes, ma'am." He motioned them to one side. "I assume you'll want underwear first?"

"Yes." That would definitely make him feel more comfortable.

"Then follow me."

They followed Brad, and Charles leaned over to whisper to Mari. "What magic did you use on him?"

She grimaced. "Kirby's platinum American Express card. I never leave home without it."

"What?"

She shook her head. "Later."

Brad turned out to be very helpful and Charles felt much better once he had undergarments on—more…supported, less as though his private parts were on display. When Charles admitted he didn't know his sizes, Brad measured him and brought different clothes to try on.

The first thing he tried on was a pair of short pants and a shirt made of something called spandex. Brad assured Charles he looked hot in them, and though he suspected Brad was using the word differently than Charles was accustomed to, he had to agree. These things made him perspire—and they were even tighter than Kirby's sweats.

When he turned to Mari, she blushed again, saying, "You probably won't need those."

Charles agreed. He didn't need anything that made Mari uncomfortable. And he didn't trust Brad's taste in clothes. Instead, Charles took matters into his own hands and searched for clothes that suited *him*.

He found just what he was looking for—faded jeans, a comfortable shirt and a black leather vest with matching black boots and hat. He tried them on and sauntered out of the dressing room. Hitching his thumbs in his belt, Charles nodded at his reflection in satisfaction. This was more like it.

He glanced at Mari for her reaction, but she merely

stood there gaping at him. "Is something wrong?" he asked.

"No, I, uh...it's definitely you."

Charles grinned and touched one finger to his hat. "Thank you, ma'am. Can we go now?"

She averted her gaze. "Not quite yet. I think you'll need a few more things."

He continued to wear the items he'd chosen while she bought him some fancier clothes and all the accessories she and Brad thought they'd need. Finally Mari pronounced them finished and paid for their purchases. They left, a smiling Brad escorting them out the door and encouraging them to come back soon.

They placed all the packages in the car and Mari said, "Well, I don't know about you, but I'm hungry. Shall we eat?"

Charles agreed, and they walked down the street to a restaurant. He stared at the menu and frowned, not really seeing anything on it.

"What's wrong?" Mari asked, interrupting his reverie.

"I just realized—with that small card, you commanded a great deal of respect. Without it, Brad probably would have ignored us."

"Well, he might not have been as attentive, anyway." She looked puzzled. "What's your point?"

"I just learned something about myself. Respect is important to me."

"It is to most people."

He frowned. "Yes, I know, but it's *very* important to me."

"And that...bothers you?"

"I'm not sure. I just thought it might make your job more difficult."

"How?"

"I'm wondering if that's why I turned to a life of crime."

"Because you didn't have respect?"

"Yes. Money generates instant respect in most people, wouldn't you say?"

"Unfortunately, yes. We just saw proof of it."

"That's right. Well, what if I started stealing to get it?"

"Do you think that's possible?"

He shrugged. "Perhaps. I don't know. I don't want to know. And therein lies the problem."

"How is that a problem?"

"If I really am the type of person who would abandon a family, then steal for a living, how can I respect myself?"

"Maybe you had a good reason—"

"No." He cut her off. "That's wishful thinking. Frankly I'd prefer not to remember my previous life at all."

A stricken look crossed Mari's face, but she quickly hid it.

"What's wrong?" He hadn't meant to upset her.

"If you won't remember, then everything is all messed up. You might as well have stayed in the past, for all the good it'll do me."

"This wasn't my idea," he reminded her gently.

"I know," she conceded, her head down. She glanced up at him, and dashed a tear from her eye. "We jerked you out of your own time and didn't even ask your permission. You have every right to refuse to help me."

The sadness in her face made him feel empty inside. He might be a rogue, but if he could help it he wouldn't be a cad. Mari wanted so much to belong somewhere. Was that so wrong?

Just then, the events of the day struck him like a blow. The sights, sounds, smells...everything was so different, so alien, that he felt totally out of place. Out of his own time, his own place, he, too, felt at a loss, as if he were on the outside looking in. He could understand Mari's feelings precisely.

She and Kirby could solve his problem by sending him back through time, but there was no such magical solution for Mari. He couldn't let her go through this for the rest of her life—not if he had the means to help her find a place where she belonged. And if Jordan was what she wanted, so be it.

He smiled at her and covered her hand with his. "Don't worry. If it's at all possible, I'll help you."

Mari's face brightened and she smiled, bringing sunshine into the room. "Thank you," she said simply.

It was the best reward he could have possibly been given. In the short time he'd known her, this woman had wrapped herself around his heart, and he knew he'd have a very hard time doing anything that would disappoint her.

He frowned. The only problem was...would he still feel this way once he regained his memory?

Chapter Four

Mari signaled to the waitress to indicate they were ready to order. The pretty young blonde hurried over to their table and flashed them a smile. Then, taking a good look at Charles, her grin widened and she gave him a saucy wink.

Charles grinned and winked back.

Mari glanced at him in surprise and really looked at him. She'd been thinking of him only as Black Bart and a distant relative, and she hadn't really noticed how very attractive he was.

Who was she kidding? His rugged sexiness would put movie cowboys to shame. She'd noticed, all right. She just hadn't realized other women would, too. No wonder the waitress was flirting with him.

The waitress chuckled and asked, "What'll you have?"

Charles's grin deepened and he leaned forward to stare into her eyes. "I don't know. What do you have to offer?"

Mari watched the byplay with a bit of envy, as Charles flirted and discussed the merits of various meals with the waitress. Why couldn't Mari be that free and easy with people? The waitress made it look simple, and she and Charles looked like they were having so much fun. If Mari could do that, she wouldn't worry so much about belonging.

She ordered, then frowned down at the table. But she didn't have to worry about belonging anymore. Charles had agreed to help her. The question was, why wasn't she happy about it? She was getting what she wanted, wasn't she?

The waitress left and Mari glanced at Charles, who tilted lazily back in his chair to survey the surroundings with an intent gaze. Sure, she was getting what she wanted, but at his expense. She usually wasn't so selfish, but the goal of belonging was finally within her grasp. All she had to do was reform this rogue, send him back in time, and she'd have everything she had ever wanted.

Her stomach roiled in protest and she put down her water glass with a grimace.

"What's wrong?" Charles asked, leaning forward again.

"I can't let you do it."

"Can't let me do what?"

Mari took a deep breath. "I can't let you help me."

The look on Charles's face was almost comical as his forehead furrowed in an attempt to understand her.

"I'm being selfish. I understand why you don't want to know about your former life. I won't make you."

"So you plan to call off your engagement?"

He sounded too happy about the prospect. Mari shot him an exasperated glance. "No, of course not. I don't give up that easily. I'll just...find another way to make his parents accept me."

"Do you really think you can accomplish that?"

Could she? "That's my problem. I should've never brought you into it."

Charles covered her hand with his. "But I wish to do this for you."

Confused by the warmth his touch generated in her, Mari jerked her hand away, knocking her water glass over in the process. She righted it, muttering, "I'm such a klutz."

"No matter. No harm done."

The water spill was irrelevant, but… "That's where you're wrong. We *have* done harm—we brought you out of your own time to a place you know nothing about and where you can't even remember your own name. How can you say we've done no harm?"

"Perhaps you've done good, in ridding the world of Black Bart."

"Oh, no, how can you say that? You've been nothing but nice and sweet since you've arrived."

"You're easy to be nice to, Mari," he said with a lazy smile. "You're so sweet yourself."

Mari felt her cheeks heat and just stared at him. She never knew how to respond to statements like that. Not that she heard them often…

Charles added softly, "And perhaps you find me kind because I have no memory of my former self. I'm learning what sort of man I am bit by bit—making it up as I go along."

"Maybe. Maybe not. But if you want, we can try to find out more about you."

"How?"

"Well, Kirby is researching methods of restoring your memory. Maybe he's learned something that will help. That is, if you really want to know." She glanced at him anxiously, wanting this to be *his* decision.

A faraway expression came over Charles's face, then hardened into decisiveness. "Yes, I need to know what sort of person I am...one way or the other. If I am Black Bart, perhaps I can change—especially with the knowledge I have now." He flashed a smile at her. "And still assist you."

Mari smiled back at him, glad he'd made the decision on his own.

After they ate lunch, they hurried back to the house and found Kirby in the garage-turned-lab, peering at the computer screen with his usual intensity. Mari smiled. This was typical of Kirby at his most focused—glasses askew, hair uncombed, and clothes rumpled.

Miraculously they were able to get his attention right away. Of course she had to turn off his computer monitor to do it, but she didn't quibble at the method if it worked.

Kirby blinked at them. "What's up?" He peered at Charles more closely. "Oh, I see you got some clothes. Good."

He reached out to switch the monitor back on, but Mari forestalled him. "That's right, but that's not why we're here. Did you have any luck finding out how to restore Charles's memory?"

"Memory..." Kirby murmured as he obviously searched his. "Hmm, yes. There isn't much written on the subject, but what I did find is that memory seems to be tied to the senses."

Charles moved a few electronic parts off a nearby chair and sat, leaning toward Kirby with an intent expression. "The senses? How?"

"Well, memory recall is triggered most strongly by the sense of smell or taste."

Charles had a doubtful look on his face. "That's interesting, but I don't know how useful it is. We could experiment with different smells and tastes for a rather long time and never hit on one that evokes a useful memory."

Kirby regarded Charles in surprise and Mari grinned to herself. She knew that expression—Kirby had become so involved in the research he had forgotten it had a very practical application.

"Oh, right," Kirby said. "Well, sights and sounds can be almost as effective, if you find the right ones."

"Again," Charles said, "how do we know which sights and sounds will be effective?"

"You could start by researching your earlier life to see where you lived, how you spent your time, that kind of thing."

Mari exchanged a glance with Charles. "That's just what we'd planned to do—check out the library."

"Well, then," Kirby said, sounding miffed, "why did you ask me?"

"Because you're a hotshot scientist. I thought maybe you'd find some kind of treatment or drug or something that would help."

"I only had a few hours," he exclaimed. "Besides, I was working on something else. Trust me, this is more important."

"What else?" Mari demanded. "What's more important than helping Charles regain his memory?"

"Well, I placed some sensors at the base of the rocks, just to track any changes that might have occurred as a result of bringing Charles through time. And...I spotted an anomaly in the field."

She didn't like the sound of that. "What kind of anomaly?"

"That's what I've been trying to find out."

Suddenly apprehensive, she asked, "What did you learn?"

"Ever since Charles...arrived, the vortexes have been acting funny—especially the one at Courthouse Rock."

"Funny how?"

"Funny peculiar."

Mari rolled her eyes. "I didn't think you meant amusing. Come on, Kirby. Spit it out. What's wrong?"

"Well, our use of the vortex as a conduit through time seems to have set up a strange resonance in the time continuum."

Charles leaned forward and fixed Kirby with a piercing stare. "What are you saying?"

"Strange forces are at work in the vortex." Kirby flipped his monitor on and turned it so they could see it. "Here, let me show you."

He glanced up at Charles and said, "Uh, this is a computer."

Though Kirby's explanation was vague in the extreme, Charles nodded, no doubt just wanting him to get on with the important information.

Kirby punched a few keys. "This is a representation of the Courthouse Rock and Bell Rock vortexes a few weeks ago. The light blue lines represent the energy flow."

Mari stared at the image on the screen. Blue eddies of energy swirled to and fro around the base of the rocks in a monotonous, soothing pattern. "And now?"

Kirby hit another key. "This is how it looks now."

The currents appeared stronger, more violent. They moved swiftly like a storm at sea, smashing impatiently into one another. Wherever they hit, they spurted high into the air and rebounded with renewed force.

Charles frowned at the monitor. "It looks angry."

Kirby nodded. "That's about the size of it."

"Angry?" Mari repeated incredulously. "You mean the vortex is mad at us?"

"Well, while I hesitate to personify—"

"Cut the jargon, Kirby. Try to explain in words of one syllable, willya?"

Kirby hesitated. "Okay. It's not the vortex so much as it is Time." The capital letter was evident in the way he emphasized the word.

"You make Time sound like a person," Charles said, echoing her thoughts.

"Well, not a person," Kirby hedged. "More like an entity."

Charles raised an eyebrow. "I see. And this Time entity is annoyed at us?"

"Yep," Kirby agreed. "Royally ticked off."

Mari couldn't believe how calmly Charles and Kirby were accepting this. "You've got to be kidding. Do you have any idea how ridiculous that sounds?"

"Of course I do. I *am* a scientist. But trust me, no other explanation fits the facts. Though bringing a man through time expends a great deal of energy, it's insignificant compared to the whole, and it should have only caused a mild ripple in the energy flows. My use of the field shouldn't have caused these fluctuations. No, something...or some*one* is causing this."

An odd movement occurred on the screen, and Charles asked, "What's that?"

"It's a surge," Kirby explained. "I haven't quite figured out what it means yet, but I'm working on it."

Mari just shook her head in disbelief as Charles and Kirby continued to discuss the situation.

"How does this affect my circumstances?" Charles asked.

"Well, the best I can tell, Time will try to rectify the situation. Already, I can see that every time a person enters the field, the energies concentrate around that individual for a brief moment, then dissipate…almost as if the field is checking out each person who enters it to see if it's you."

"Me? Are you certain it's not searching for *you?* You caused the problem."

"Uh, good point. But I don't think it's vindictive— more like it's just trying to regain its rightful…property. But I do know it's drawing energy from the other vortexes and is extending its boundaries a little at a time, searching."

Mari couldn't believe Kirby was spouting this nonsense. Time, an intelligent entity? Yeah, right. "Well, then, we'll just stay away from the vortexes."

"It's not that simple."

"Why not?" she asked.

"Here, I'll show you." Kirby magnified the image on the screen between the two rocks. "See that thin red line coming out of the center of the flows?"

"Yes," Mari answered. It led off in a straight line, directly away from the base.

"Well, I traced that line."

"Where does it go?" she asked.

Kirby pointed at Charles. "To *him*."

"Me?" Charles repeated, staring down at himself.

"Oh, you can't see it," Kirby said. "This is just a representation. But there's no doubt about it—it's connected to you."

"But what does it portend?" Charles asked.

Kirby shrugged. "I can only hypothesize."

"So hypothesize, then," Mari said impatiently. She'd never known Kirby to be wrong, even with his guesses.

"Well, my theory is this line connects Charles to his true place in time, like a lifeline. And if the vortex gets strong enough, it might be able to tug on the connection."

Charles stared at him. "You mean Time might reel me in...like a fish?"

"I'm just guessing, mind you, but that's entirely possible. Of course if you enter the field yourself, it might not have to."

"What happens then, when I'm in the field?"

"I assume Time will send you back to your proper place."

A myriad of expressions crossed Charles's face—apprehension, fear, hope, confusion, doubt. "How long?"

"The connection stretches, depending on where you are. There seems to be no limit on how far you can go."

"No. I meant how long before...I must return?"

"Oh." Kirby turned to type in a few calculations on the computer. "Well, at the rate it's increasing now, I'd say you have a week or two before it becomes strong enough. I'll have a better idea later, when I have more data."

Mari looked at Kirby in dismay. "A week or two? Isn't there anything you can do?"

"I'm afraid not," Kirby said as Charles watched, white-faced.

Impossible. Kirby could do anything. "Can't you cut the connection?"

He shrugged. "I might be able to, but trust me, any force strong enough to sever a connection through time would also destroy Charles—and half of Sedona."

"Can't you try to find a solution that won't?" Mari demanded.

"I could, but why?"

"What do you mean, why?"

"Well," Kirby said, "don't you want to send him back? So he can change history and you can marry...whatshisname?"

Didn't she? "Yes, yes, of course. But only if Charles wants to go."

"He may not have a choice."

Obviously. "And I don't know if he'll regain his memory by then. Two weeks isn't much time."

Kirby gave her a compassionate look. "You'll just have to do your best to stimulate his senses, then."

Stimulate his senses? Mari blushed as her imagination conjured up a sensual vision. Hastily she tried to wipe the image out of her mind. Heck, she couldn't help it if she thought of him in that way. Charles was a good-looking man, and nice, too, even if his diction was a bit old-fashioned. Sure, he vacillated a bit between roguish charm and courtly manners, but that just added to his appeal.

And he was only going to be here for a couple of weeks. Besides, she reminded herself, he was Black

Bart, a notorious outlaw...and her uncle. Well, not really her uncle since he was so many generations removed and they weren't even related by blood. But the fact was, she was silly to even think about him in that way. Not to mention the fact that she was engaged to another man.

Mari sighed. If she were to stimulate his senses, it looked like it had better be in the library.

As THEY DROVE TO the lending library in the dangerous contraption Mari called a car, Charles attempted to sort through his jumble of emotions. The longer he continued without recalling anything of his past, the more rootless and unconnected he felt. This vast hole in his knowledge was frustrating and annoying.

What he'd told Mari was correct. Even if he was Black Bart, he had to know what sort of person he really was—though he hoped to prove he wasn't the scalawag Black Bart was made out to be.

He hesitated. But...what if he was?

Quite simple. He'd just have to do his utmost to ensure he reformed so he could help Mari's dream come true—even if her dream was Jordan Sloan.

Mari interrupted his thoughts. "We're here."

They entered the library and Charles looked around in awe. "So many books!"

Several people turned to glare at him, and Mari said, "Shh. We need to be quiet in here. Besides, this is nothing. This is a very small library. You should see the ones in Phoenix."

"All right," he said in a softer tone. "Where do we start?"

Mari led him to something she called a card catalog and began searching for information on Black Bart,

Wells Fargo, stagecoach robbers and his time period. They located a few references, and Mari checked them out.

When they returned to her home, she laid the books on the kitchen table and opened the door into the lab. "Kirby? Oh, there you are."

Charles followed her in as she said, "There weren't many books at the library, so I may need to borrow your computer later and check to see what's out on the Internet. Is that okay?"

"Sure," Kirby said in a distracted tone.

A small mewling sound came from the floor near Kirby's feet.

"What's that noise?" Mari bent down and retrieved a small ball of gray-and-white striped fur. Incongruously, someone had tied a blue handkerchief around its neck.

She glared at Kirby. "What's this?"

He glanced at it. "A kitten."

"I can see that." She stroked the kitten's head as it squeaked plaintively. "I didn't know you wanted a pet."

"I don't. It's part of an experiment."

From the outraged expression on Mari's face, it appeared Kirby was in for a rare trimming. She sputtered for a moment, then asked, "An *experiment?* What are you planning to do with this poor little thing?"

"Trust me, Mari. I'm not going to hurt it," Kirby reassured her. "I'm just going to send it through time."

"Oh, no, you're not," Mari said in a menacing tone. "Remember what happened to Charles? I'm not going to let you do that to an unsuspecting kitten.

Why, who knows where it would end up? It might starve to death.''

Charles regarded her with a quirked smile. She hadn't let that stop her from bringing an unsuspecting man—him—through time. Nevertheless, he couldn't fault her sentiments.

''But I'm only going to send it a day or two into the future,'' Kirby said, ''just to test the time field and see how long it'll take Time to notice and snatch it back. With the smaller time differential and the significantly lower mass of the kitten, I should be able to calculate...'' He trailed off as he glanced up at Mari's mutinous face.

Charles was hard put to restrain a smile.

''You're going to take it into *that?*'' Mari pointed at the computer screen, where the representation of the time field roiled and twisted.

''Yeah,'' Kirby said doubtfully.

''Don't you think that's a little dangerous? Charles got knocked out coming through time. Imagine what would happen to this poor little thing. It can't be more than three months old. You'll kill it for sure.'' The kitten punctuated her remark with a plaintive meow.

''See?'' Mari asked, as if the kitten had corroborated her statement. ''He's probably starving. I'll get him something to eat. You are *not* going to use this cat as a guinea pig.''

''But—'' Kirby began, to no avail. Mari was already halfway out the door.

She paused to glance down at the kitten, then back at Kirby. ''If you weren't going to keep it as a pet, why did you tie a handkerchief around its neck?''

''To find out what happened to Charles's clothes,'' Kirby explained.

Mari rolled her eyes and completed her exit. Kirby looked at Charles with a plaintive expression, much like the one the kitten had worn. "Trust me, I wasn't going to hurt it. I've calculated every variable very carefully."

Charles grinned. "I believe you. But you know how women are. Once they get a bee in their bonnet, you can never sway them. I fear you'll have to give in and find another test method."

Kirby sighed. "I guess you're right." He shook his head. "Women!" Then his gaze unfocused as he started working at the problem of finding another way to test the field.

Some things never changed. Charles chuckled and left to find Mari in the kitchen, pouring a saucer of milk for the small creature she'd rescued. Murmuring wordless sounds of comfort to it, she set the saucer down, and the kitten lapped up the milk eagerly.

He grinned, finding himself oddly touched. "How's your protégé?"

Mari smiled back, a little shamefaced. "Very hungry, I think. I don't know what Kirby was thinking." Her look defied him to disagree.

"Hmm," he said noncommittally. Discretion appeared to be most appropriate in this situation. "What are you going to do with him? Uh, it *is* a him?"

"Well, it's hard to tell at this age, but I think so. Besides, I can't call him 'it.'"

"And what are you going to do with him?" he repeated.

She raised her chin a notch. "I'm going to keep him. I've always wanted a pet. In fact, I don't know why I never got one before."

Charles couldn't help smiling.

"What?" she asked in a challenging tone.

His grin widened. "I imagine you didn't because you feared Kirby would utilize your pet in his experiments."

That surprised a laugh out of her. "You're right. But I won't let him get this little guy." She stroked the kitten on the head with her finger. "Will I, fella?"

She gazed thoughtfully at Charles. "It's almost dinnertime. Why don't I run down to the store and grab a few things he'll need, then pick up a pizza for dinner? You can get started on those books and see if anything refreshes your memory."

Pizza? What was that? "All right."

"And while I'm gone, watch after Buster here. I don't want Kirby to sneak in and make off with him."

"Buster?"

Mari blushed. "Yes. I just named him. Any problem with that?"

"No, no, none at all," Charles said, trying to suppress a smile. She looked so sweet when she blushed. On sudden impulse, he leaned forward and placed a soft kiss on her brow.

He intended it to be merely a platonic kiss between friends, but her sweet scent and intoxicating nearness were almost his undoing. He kissed her there again, more lingeringly this time, though he wanted nothing more than to move his lips lower, to capture her sweet lips or taste the fluttering pulse on the delicate line of her neck.

Mari backed away and raised shaking fingers to her temple, a stunned look on her face. "What was that for?"

"For you," he said in a husky voice. "I thought you deserved a kiss."

"Oh," she said with a panicked look, then grabbed her purse and fled out the door.

Charles stared after her, shaking his head. There were so many sides to this woman—she was clumsy, yet a fire-eater in defense of the helpless. She was shy, yet she had layers of passion waiting to be explored. If only she would stand up for herself the way she stood up for Buster. And if only Charles could be the one to explore those hidden depths.

Unfortunately that was the last thing she wanted. Sighing, he eyed the pile of books on the table. If he really wanted to help Mari, he'd better start reading.

He read until late, pausing only to eat the delicious "pizza" Mari had brought home with her. They sat on opposite chairs in the comfortable living room, both reading, with Buster curled up in Mari's lap.

As Charles read about the 1870s, he became more and more puzzled. Finally he yawned and rubbed his eyes.

Mari looked up. "Tired?" she asked.

"A little."

"Had any luck?"

"No. Everything seems somewhat familiar, yet none of it evokes any real memories of places I've been, events I've witnessed or sights I've seen." He shook his head. "I'm not certain this is the correct approach for learning my past."

"Well, maybe this will help." Mari picked up the book she'd been reading and brought it over to him. "Here's some information about Black Bart."

Trying to ignore the distraction of her nearness, Charles forced his tired eyes to read some more. He gazed at the letters before him but his eyes blurred, then focused in tight on a date. *July 26, 1875.* He checked the text. "This says I robbed my first stage-coach in 1875."

"Yes. We picked you up on that date."

"No, you didn't."

"Hmm?"

"When I woke, I distinctly remember you saying you picked me up in 1874, not 1875."

Mari glanced at him in surprise. "Are you sure?"

"I'm quite certain."

"Wait here," she said. "Let me check what date I gave Kirby."

As she went to check with Kirby, Charles continued reading about his escapades as one of the Wild West's most famous stagecoach robbers.

When Mari came back, she appeared troubled. "You're right. We did pick you up in 1874." She brightened. "You know what that means?"

"No, what?"

"Maybe we got the wrong guy. Since we got there a year earlier, who knows whom we might have picked up? Maybe you're not Black Bart after all."

"I don't think—"

"No, really. Think about it. We knew Black Bart was at that place in 1875, but that doesn't mean he was there when we picked you up. In fact, the odds are against it. You aren't him," she finished on an enthusiastic note.

"I'm afraid that's merely wishful thinking."

"No, it's not."

"Yes, it is," Charles said firmly. "I finally remembered something."

"What?"

He glanced down at the page. "They called Black Bart the gentleman poet. Here's a poem he wrote. I haven't read it yet, but I know precisely what it says."

He handed it to her and recited it, watching her mouth drop open in disbelief. "So, did I recite it correctly?"

"Word for word. Are you sure you didn't memorize it just now?"

Charles shook his head. "No. I read only the first line."

"How is this possible?"

"I must have lived near there, investigated the robbery site, even a year earlier. Whatever the reason, it doesn't matter. I remembered the poem."

He hesitated, unwilling to voice the words that would confirm his identity. "I must indeed be Black Bart."

Chapter Five

The next morning, Charles entered the kitchen to find Mari playing with the kitten. She glanced up at him with an apprehensive expression. "Good morning. How are you?"

He knew her question was much more than a query after his well-being. What she was trying not to say was, "How do you feel knowing you really are Black Bart, notorious stagecoach robber?" and, "Now that you've started to remember, are you going to turn into a monster?"

Not knowing the answer to either question, he grunted a noncommittal reply and accepted the cup of coffee she handed him. He sipped appreciatively. He'd only been here a short time, and already she knew just how he liked it—black and strong.

Abandoning the kitten, Mari joined him at the table with her cup of tea. Charles raised his head and gave her a small smile, just to reassure her he hadn't turned into a beast overnight.

"Did you remember any more?" she asked.

"No." He'd gone to bed immediately after the revelation the previous night, not having the stomach to continue with his investigation.

"Are you okay?"

The genuine concern in her voice touched him. "Yes, but..."

"But?" she prompted.

"I didn't realize it until last night, but I rather hoped I would turn out to be someone else. Anyone but Black Bart."

"I know. I—I think I did, too."

Mari surprised him by covering his hand with hers. He didn't know why it surprised him—she was compassionate enough for three people. She was only shy and bashful until someone needed her help, and then she turned fiercely protective, like a tigress defending her young.

He turned his palm upward and clasped her hand in his. It helped. This small comfort soothed him, made him feel more as if he had an ally, so he wouldn't have to face the world alone.

Mari gave his hand a light squeeze. "Are you still willing to let me reform you?"

"Yes, of course. But..."

"But?"

"But I don't really feel as if I need reforming." Except maybe for the way he was beginning to think about *her*. But that wasn't the point.

"I don't understand. You agreed you are Black Bart—or you will be, I mean. Do you *want* to be a notorious outlaw?"

"No, no. I'm saying that I—the me I am right now—doesn't need reformation. I'm not Black Bart yet."

"I know that—"

"And I don't remember enough of my past to understand why I would take to a life of crime. Until I learn that, we won't know what it would take to have you reform me.''

"I see," Mari said. "Well, are you willing to continue your research, then?"

As little as he wanted to learn more, he knew he had to. He needed to understand what forces had driven him to abandon a family, to steal. Oh, he didn't expect to justify his crimes, but he had to know—as a means toward change. Not only to help Mari, but to bring his conduct and mores in line with what he believed was his true nature.

"Yes," he answered simply. "I'll continue the research."

"Good. Well, our small library didn't seem to have much. Why don't we check out the Internet? Kirby said we could use his computer."

Charles wasn't sure what she was talking about, but if Mari thought it would help, he was willing to play along. He followed her into Kirby's lab, Buster darting along behind him. He glanced down at the kitten in amusement. If the cat knew what was good for him, he'd stay well out of Kirby's reach—and away from any scientific apparatus.

Lucky Buster—Kirby wasn't in the lab. Mari sat in front of the computer and turned the machine on, placing the insistent kitten in her lap. He appeared content, though a bit puzzled as he blinked and watched the images on the screen in fascination.

Charles chuckled and took a seat near her. He knew just how the cat felt. "What are you doing?"

"The Internet connects us to different computer systems all over the world. We can view any file they let us have access to, plus any that other people have developed in their individual net space to advertise products or collect information about a certain subject. I'm hoping one of them will have data on you.''

"I see." It was no exaggeration—he found her explanation easy to understand. "So to learn about one particular subject, I assume there is some way to search for the information we want? Like the card catalog at the library?"

She looked at him in surprise. "Exactly. You catch on quickly. Here, let me show you. We'll do a search." Her fingers flew over the board as she typed in his alias. "Now we wait while the system looks for Black Bart. If there's anything out there on you, it'll show up as a match."

Charles was surprised at how easily he was able to grasp these concepts, feeling a bit of pride that he understood something so complex that was clearly not from his own time.

When the screen changed, Mari's eyebrows rose. "There are a lot of matches. Good—let's see what we have here."

Each "match" had a short description following it, but most of them seemed to have just the word "black" or "Bart" in them. Some had both, but most centered around something called Bart Simpson's blackboard.

"Who's Bart Simpson?" he asked.

"A television character. And before you ask, I'm not going to explain television—you have enough to deal with during the short time you're here without being exposed to *that* madness."

She glared at the screen. "Well, this isn't going to help. Let me try a different search engine and be more specific."

Quite a few matches showed up again, but this time

all of them had the name Black Bart in them. Mari investigated each one, though many of them seemed to be nothing but establishments that had appropriated his name for the purpose of advertising.

It seemed odd to find hotels, furniture stores and sundry other businesses named after him. "Why do these people believe association with an outlaw will enhance their business?"

"Well, Black Bart was a very popular outlaw...with everyone but Wells Fargo. According to this abstract, he—you—committed almost thirty robberies, but your gun was never loaded."

"But I haven't committed them yet."

"Talking about time travel is confusing, isn't it? Well, unless we restore your memory and reform you, this *will* be your future. Anyway, you sort of became a symbol of the common man's rebellion against authority, especially since you thumbed your nose at the establishment by not using bullets and by leaving poems at your robberies."

Well, he wasn't all bad, then. Maybe he wasn't as bad as he'd originally thought. He shook his head. "Yet another instance where people are impressed by nefarious deeds." He was beginning to think the rest of society was in the wrong, not him, for advocating such chicanery.

"Odd, isn't it?" she agreed. "Well, I guess that'll do it." She turned off the machine. "I have the names of a few more books that might help. Our library could probably get them on interlibrary loan, but it'll be much faster to drive down to Phoenix and check out the libraries there."

"All right—"

A loud ringing noise startled him. What was that?

Oh, yes, the telephone. He still wasn't used to these noisy interruptions.

Mari went into the kitchen to answer it and Charles followed her. Apparently it was Jordan. Charles tuned out the conversation, not wanting to intrude or hear anything to do with the lukewarm man Mari planned to marry.

Jordan didn't seem to appreciate just how special Mari was. What did she see in him anyway? Charles pondered the puzzle for a moment, then finally concluded it must be because Jordan gave her attention. From the little Charles had seen of her, it was plain that Mari was starved for affection, even if she wasn't aware of it.

But when she did receive it, she didn't know how to deal with it—as evidenced by the manner in which she had responded to his simple kiss last night. A sudden thought struck him. If she responded to him and not her own fiancé, perhaps Jordan wasn't doing it right.

Charles's jaw clenched. Damn the man—he just wasn't good enough for Mari. But it wasn't Charles's place to tell her who she could marry.

Mari hung up the phone. "That was Jordan."

"Yes?"

She twisted her hands, giving him a tremulous smile. "He's invited me to dinner to meet his parents."

She looked so abject, he couldn't help asking, "Isn't that what you wanted?"

"Yes, I suppose." She hesitated, then said, "He stood up for me. Told them I was his girlfriend and that it was silly to dislike me because of Black Bart."

Because of me. Regret surged through him. Damn,

he didn't want to hurt her—either now or in the future. "That's good, isn't it?" From the expression on her face, he wasn't certain.

"Yes, but..." Her face crumpled into uncertainty and she resumed her seat, gesturing awkwardly, almost knocking over her cup.

"What is it, Mari?" he asked gently. He hated seeing her like this.

She twisted her hands again and her words came out in a rush, tumbling all over each other. "I—I don't have anything to wear, I'm a total klutz, I don't know how to act in front of them, I'm going to make a fool of myself—and they've invited my *parents,*" she wailed.

His heart went out to her, and he pulled her from her seat to gather her in his arms. She sobbed on his shoulder and he tried to provide what comfort he could. "Shh, everything is going to be just fine."

She just sobbed harder, but leaned into the comfort he offered. He held her, surprised at how protective he felt. He wanted to take on the world for her, shield her from abhorrent prospective in-laws and uncaring fiancés. But she didn't need that—she just wanted comfort. Wordlessly, he gave it to her.

Finally, her tears spent, she backed away, sniffling. "I—I'm sorry. I didn't mean to dump on you." She grabbed a tissue and blew her nose.

"That's all right. Why don't we sit down and take these problems one at a time?" They reseated themselves, and Mari clutched her cup as if it were a lifeline.

"First, we can always buy you something to wear," he said.

"Yes, but—"

"And you don't have to act differently around Jordan's parents. Just be yourself."

"Be myself? Gee, thanks. I'm a total klutz, and you want me to be myself? That'll ruin everything."

"Klutz?"

"Yeah. You know—clumsy, awkward, ungainly...totally inept. Me."

"It seems to me you're only clumsy when you're nervous."

"Well, that doesn't help. I won't be able to help being nervous around the Sloans. They're so..."

"Full of themselves? Snobbish?"

Mari grinned. "I don't know, I haven't met them yet. But I was thinking elegant, refined."

"You are elegant and refined, too, you know."

"Yeah, right."

"I *am* right. When you lose your nervousness, you are graceful and poised. All we have to do is give you some confidence."

"In two days?"

"We can try, can't we? I'll help. Now, about that last problem. I thought your parents were away on a trip."

"They are, but they'll be back sometime tonight. Jordan knew that."

"And why are they a problem?"

"I love my parents, but they're not in the same league as the Sloans. I'm afraid the Sloans may snub them, and I really don't want them to get hurt that way."

This problem was a little tougher. "I'm not certain—"

"And my parents have this tendency to brag about

being descended from Black Bart—you—every time they meet someone new."

"Can't you explain the situation to them and ask them to refrain?"

"Yes, but I don't want to hurt their feelings."

"That's commendable," Charles said, "but you can't have it both ways."

Her expression turned mulish. "I can if they don't go."

"That's true. You could make up some excuse for them, but don't you want their support?"

Mari worried her lower lip between her teeth. "I suppose."

"And they are bound to meet the Sloans sooner or later, if you plan to marry Jordan. Why not make it sooner?"

Her shoulders slumped. "I guess you're right."

"Don't worry, I'll assist you. You'll come through this just fine."

"But what about the library? Your research?"

"That can wait."

"But your memory—"

"This comes first. The only reason I am trying to regain my memory is so you can reform me—so your fiancé's parents won't dismiss you out of hand. But if you become, as you say, a 'klutz', that will give them all the more reason to reject you. You don't want that, do you?"

"No, of course not."

"So our aim should be to give you enough confidence to weather this dinner party." Even if it did mean ensuring she married Jordan.

Mari cringed as she thought about everything that could go wrong. It didn't matter what Charles thought—she knew she was going to screw it up. "How are you going to do that?"

"The first thing we need to do is find out what's causing your problem."

"For heaven's sake, you sound like a pop psychologist." Then, realizing he probably wouldn't understand that word, she clarified, "Someone who studies people and how they act."

He gave her an odd look. "It's just common sense. If we can find out what's causing it and correct that, then it will be easier to treat the problem itself."

"But I know what the problem is. I'm just shy. It's my nature—there's no cause for it."

"Perhaps, but let us take a different approach and look at when you're shy and when you're not. For example, I've noticed you're very comfortable with Kirby. You're not shy with him."

"But that's because I've known him since third grade."

"I understand, but I've also noticed you were fearless when it came to the defense of young Buster."

"Well, someone had to stick up for him."

"Precisely my point. You lose your reserve when you know someone well, or in defending those less fortunate than yourself or in need of championing."

"So how does this help?" Mari asked in exasperation. "I don't know the Sloans and won't until the dinner party. And I can't think of a single guest who'll need me to stick up for them."

"Perhaps," Charles said, with an enigmatic smile, "but I have some ideas along those lines I'll put to you later. For now, let's concentrate on making you comfortable with me."

From the roguish twinkle in his eye, Mari wasn't

at all sure she was going to like this. "What do you mean?"

"You're wary of me. I can't help you unless you lose your shyness and become more comfortable."

Easily said, but how did he plan to accomplish it?

He cocked his head and eyed her with a smile. "Why do I intimidate you? Is it because I'm going to become Black Bart?"

How could he think that? "No, of course not. Oh, maybe at first, but I can tell you're nowhere near as bad as the Sloans and others have painted you."

"Then what? I'm your great-great-something uncle. A relative, even if it's not by blood. That should make you feel more secure."

"Maybe it should, but it doesn't." If they really were related, she wouldn't feel this surge of... awareness every time he came near her. If she were honest with herself, she'd call it attraction—a heavy attraction. She could still remember the thrill she'd felt from just his simple kiss on her forehead. What would happen if—

She pushed the thought aside. Charles was only going to be here a week or two, and then he'd be gone forever. Besides, there was Jordan. Mari berated herself—she shouldn't have to continually remind herself of her fiancé's existence.

Charles interrupted her musings. "You're doing it again."

"What?"

"You're retreating inside yourself. Look at your arms."

Mari looked down. Sometime in the past few minutes, she had wrapped her arms around her middle. Quickly she unfolded them and let them hang awkwardly at her side.

"You see?" Charles asked. "You do it every time you feel uncomfortable. Something I said made you feel that way. What was it?"

Oh, no. She wasn't about to tell him *that*. She shrugged and twisted her fingers together, still not knowing what to do with her hands. "Uh, you don't *feel* like a relative, you know."

"Then let's remedy that. Displays of affection disturb you, don't they?"

"I suppose." Where was he going with this?

"You retreat inside yourself whenever I touch you or speak of something close to you. So, we'll just have to accustom you to that."

Wary now, she asked, "What do you mean?"

He stood and held out his hand. "Come, I'll show you."

She was tempted as hell. Too tempted. When she hesitated, he smiled, saying, "It's all right. Trust me."

She giggled a little hysterically. "Now you sound like Kirby."

"Then you haven't any reason to fear me, have you?"

"I—I guess not." She placed her hand in his, and followed with more than a little reluctance as he led her out of the kitchen and into the living room. She tripped over the rug in the hallway and shrugged apologetically when Charles turned to see what was wrong.

Sheesh. Nothing like confirming his diagnosis.

He smiled, then seated them both on the couch. "Now, isn't this more comfortable?"

She murmured noncommittally. She found her living room, decorated in early Sears and Roebuck, very comfortable, though the Sloans would probably sneer at its lack of a cohesive style. It suited her though, which was all that mattered. But that wasn't what Charles was asking, and she knew it.

No, she wasn't comfortable, especially since he was still holding her hand. She kept this room darkened to keep it cool, but now she regretted it. In the dim light, their clasped hands seemed too...intimate. She tried to tug hers away, but he held it fast.

"Relax," he crooned. "I'm not going to hurt you. Just think of me as...a good friend."

A good friend? He had to be kidding. No friend of hers was as sexy as this guy.

Damn, there was that word again. She could feel her cheeks flush as she remembered how he'd looked the first time she'd seen him. She couldn't relax, not when he was so near and she was thinking of him in that way. If anything, she became even stiffer.

Charles sighed. "This isn't going to work. It appears I need to employ more drastic measures." He reached out and pulled her crossways into his lap, his arms now firmly around her waist.

Shocked, she froze, not knowing how to react. What was he doing? She sat stiff as a board in his embrace, overly conscious of the warmth of his body stealing into hers, the soft exhalation of his breath on her neck and his musky masculine aroma.

"It's all right, I'm not going to hurt you," he said in a low, sexy voice that made her feel all puddly inside. "I'm just going to hold you. Pretend you're crying on my shoulder again. That wasn't so difficult, was it?"

"No," she said in a small voice. She'd needed the comfort then, and had thought of him as nothing more than a pillow to cry on. But now it was different. She couldn't help but notice the shape and contours of this pillow—and they were all man.

He rubbed the small of her back and gave her a reassuring smile. "Come, now, lay your head on my shoulder."

He wasn't going to quit until she gave in. Realizing this, Mari sighed and laid her head on his shoulder, trying to relax. She wanted to cooperate but was afraid to give in to her feelings.

He continued rubbing her back and some of her tension eased. It was cozy here and very seductive. She wanted nothing more than to sink into him, to let him take all her cares away. She missed being held, being comforted...being loved. And why shouldn't she be? Just for a few minutes, why not? She let her muscles loosen.

"That's it," Charles murmured. "See, that isn't so difficult after all. Now let's just sit this way for a while, shall we?"

Mari murmured her assent and cuddled into Charles's embrace, one arm curled against his side as the other curved around his neck. A languid warmth stole through her, making her limbs limp and weak. She nestled her head even more comfortably on his shoulder and let her arm trail down his solid chest until it lay quite naturally at his waist. Feeling a little drowsy, Mari closed her eyes and let her mind wander where it would.

She slipped into one of her favorite daydreams, the one where she was beautiful and sophisticated, a leader in the best social circles. Her guests had just left, and she and her husband were curled up together on their beautiful matching living-room set as he praised her social grace and skill.

Jordan had always featured prominently in these dreams in the past, but she was finding this reality much more pleasant than her imagination…except in one respect. If this were her dream, this is the moment when Jordan would raise her chin and kiss her—a long, lingering slow kiss that promised to fulfill her every desire.

Right on cue, Charles smoothed the heavy fall of hair from her brow and kissed her on the temple. As he continued to massage her back and arm with his gentle hands, Mari almost melted into a puddle of pure need. This felt so good, so right.

Remembering the waitress and how much fun she'd had, Mari decided to try a little flirting herself. Tentatively she returned his caresses, letting her hand glide up his hard chest to come to rest curved around his neck, fondling the soft hair at his nape.

He dropped another kiss on her forehead and Mari decided to return the favor. Opening her eyes, she saw that the strong line of his neck was in easy reach, only an inch away. She placed a kiss there, at the soft skin just below his hairline.

Charles's arms tightened around her as he inhaled sharply. Encouraged, Mari repeated the kiss, letting it linger as she held his head sandwiched between her lips and her caressing hand.

"Mari?" Charles asked in an uncertain voice. But his hands were far from uncertain as he cradled her even closer, both arms wrapped around her as if she were his lover.

"Mmm," she said, submerged in the sensations his

nearness brought her. A melting warmth formed wherever their bodies touched, as if their flesh were trying to meld together. Small thrills of excitement shivered through her, making moisture pool between her legs and her breasts peak in response.

Heaven, sheer heaven. Knowing she could trust Charles, she indulged her senses fully and rubbed her breasts against his chest, wondering if she dared raise her mouth to his.

Charles's caressing hands stilled for a moment as he said in a low voice, "I don't think this is quite proper."

What an odd thing for a rogue to say. She tilted her head back, letting her eyes remain half lidded. Their lips so close they were almost touching, she stared into his eyes in the darkened room and whispered, "Why not? Isn't this what you wanted?"

What he wanted was obvious, as the evidence of his desire pressed against her thigh. She wanted to turn in his embrace, to nestle her hips against his. Could she be so provocative, so bold?

As she contemplated it, their lips only a breath apart, Charles said, "This isn't...precisely...what I had...planned." But as if he couldn't help it, he brushed his lips against hers in a fleeting kiss.

Now that was more like it. A thrill raced through her and she deepened the kiss, wanting more.

He jerked away, saying, "Ow!"

Ow? "What's wrong?"

He leaned over to pluck Buster from his pants and hand the kitten to her. "He's trying to climb my leg with those razor claws of his."

Saddened that the mood had been broken, Mari settled back into Charles's embrace. She cuddled the kitten to her, though she felt more like scolding him. Buster seemed entirely too satisfied with himself.

Charles cast her a wary look. "I don't think—"

"That's all right, don't think. I understand." She did understand—neither of them had intended this intimacy, yet it had happened. She couldn't say she was sorry. He had made her feel more alive than she had felt in years. "You were right."

Charles still held her loosely in his arms, though his clenched fists showed he was trying hard to keep his hands from caressing her. "About what?"

"You did make me feel more self-confident." Boy, did he ever. She didn't know where this side of her had come from, but she rather liked it. It made her feel warm and loved. Special.

But that was over now and Charles appeared to be very uncomfortable. Reluctantly she slid off his lap onto the couch next to him.

He breathed a sigh of relief. "Uh, yes, I believe you're right. Perhaps this is the wrong approach. Have you, uh, ever tried this with…Jordan?"

Jordan? *No, I've never felt like this with Jordan.* To be fair, she added, *Yet.* Jordan felt that man should learn to control his animal passion. He controlled his admirably, and had rarely given Mari more than a chaste peck. "No, Jordan's never asked me to sit on his lap."

Charles gave her a funny look. "Then perhaps you should take the initiative."

She grinned. "Maybe I will." But the thought wasn't as appealing as it should have been. She couldn't picture Jordan cuddling. Instead, all she could imagine was his frozen look of horror. "But I don't think the dinner party is the time to do that, do you?'' she teased.

Charles chuckled. "Perhaps not. But...are you comfortable with Jordan?"

"Yes, of course. Why?"

"Well, if you are, then perhaps you can ask him what topics of conversation are likely to come up. Let him know your discomfort. Perhaps he can help you."

She pierced him with a look. "Are you copping out on me?"

"I beg your pardon?"

"I thought you were going to help me."

"Oh, I am," Charles assured her. "But can't Jordan help, too?"

She hated to admit it, but... She bent her head to stroke Buster's soft fur. "Jordan doesn't quite understand my problem. He thinks I just need to ignore it and it will go away. He can't understand why the thought of meeting his parents makes me so nervous." In defense of her fiancé, she added, "He's a misfit, too, remember? Just...in a different way."

"Then we'll have to take another approach," Charles said. "Do you love Jordan enough to fight for him?"

"Why, yes." Wasn't that what this time-travel business was all about?

"Then fight for him—fight for the two of you— just as you fought for Buster."

"Fight?" The concept was intriguing, but she needed to hear more.

"Not physically. What I mean is, think of your marriage to Jordan as being in danger or under attack from the Sloans. I'll wager if you do, you'll find it easy to maintain your self-confidence in fighting them off.''

Her hopes rose. "You think so?"

"I'm certain of it."

Mari grinned. It might just work.

Chapter Six

Charles found it difficult to make it through the rest of the afternoon and evening. Each time he glanced at Mari, he recalled how she had curled into him, trusting him. And how she had felt in his arms—warm, soft and very right.

But that way lay madness. He had enough black marks against his soul already without adding any more. He was married, even if he couldn't remember his wife and family, and Mari was engaged. Perhaps he was more like Black Bart than he thought. Disgusted with himself, he did his best to keep his distance.

Mari cooperated. She'd emerged from the experience rather smug and self-satisfied, but that progressed to a mild embarrassment over the course of the day—as evidenced by her increasing clumsiness.

Charles regretted ever beginning her education. He'd expected to increase her self-confidence, not add to her problems. If he couldn't be with her in the way he craved, he wanted her to be comfortable with him—so he could enjoy the same sort of teasing camaraderie she shared with Kirby.

Vowing to find ways to help, not hinder her, he

went to bed and woke with a plan. As usual, he found Mari in the kitchen.

"Good morning," he said with forced cheerfulness. "I've been thinking."

"Oh?"

"Yes. As the saying goes, clothes make the man...or in this case, the woman. Being properly dressed for an occasion makes you feel confident, more in command of the situation. Shall we review your wardrobe to find such a dress for tomorrow evening?"

Mari grimaced. "That won't be necessary. I know I don't have anything suitable to wear. I don't get out much, and when I do it's usually casual."

Just as he'd expected. "Well, then, turnabout's fair play. We shall visit the local merchants to locate a suitable dress."

"But—"

"I won't hear any objections. You need a dress to make you feel more assured tomorrow night, so a dress you shall have." Before she could formulate any more objections, he said, "Find your purse and keys, and bring that little silver card with you. I need to talk to Kirby for a moment, then we'll go."

Satisfied he had done as much as he could, Charles joined Mari in the kitchen. "Are you ready?"

"Yes, but—"

"Then we shall leave." He wasn't going to give her the chance to change her mind. She needed this, and he was determined she should have it.

"Where are we going?"

"That's up to you. What is the best dress shop in town?"

"Well, there are a lot of them..."

"But which do you like best?"

"There is one..."

"Good. Then that's where we'll go."

"But it's so expensive."

"Nonsense. You can afford it, can't you?" He knew she could. Kirby had informed him that she rarely spent her generous salary.

"Well, yes, but do you think I should be spending my money on something so frivolous?"

Charles escorted her out the door. "Don't think of it as frivolity. Think of it as an investment in your future."

"All right." She sounded doubtful, but obediently entered the car and headed downtown.

They stopped in front of a women's clothing store and Charles was pleased to see that Mari had followed his instructions. If the elegant merchandise in the window was any indication, this establishment would have just what they sought.

Mari must have been here before, for she went to one particular rack and pulled out a dress. The look on her face was full of longing as she smoothed the folds of the garment.

"Go ahead," Charles urged. "Try it on."

Mari flashed him a smile, then followed a waiting clerk to a dressing room. While she was changing, Charles wandered around the establishment, selecting a few other garments for her consideration.

When Mari emerged from the dressing room, he smiled. It was true—clothes did make the woman. The dress was simplicity itself but the lines hugged her slender figure to perfection, giving her curves and making her look infinitely feminine...infinitely desirable.

The royal blue color was perfect, too, adding a glow to her complexion and making her eyes appear wide and sparkling. Around the lump in his throat, he managed to say, "You look beautiful."

Mari's mouth widened in a delighted smile. "You really think so? It's not too plain?"

Her delight was enchanting. He smiled. "Absolutely not. It makes you look elegant and sophisticated."

She smiled. "I've wanted this dress for a long time, but I wasn't sure..."

"Buy it," Charles advised. Her instincts as to what suited her were sound. This was going to be easier than he thought. "Here, try these."

She glanced down at the clothes he handed her in confusion. "But what about the dress I'm wearing?"

"Buy it," Charles repeated. "But you're going to need another dress for Kirby's birthday dance, aren't you?"

Enlightenment dawned on her face. "You're right. I will." She smiled, apparently happy at the thought that someone had given her permission—almost ordered her, really—to spend money on herself. She took the clothing he offered and went back into the dressing room.

None of them quite worked, until she tried on a dress in a deep wine color. Charles couldn't help but inhale in appreciation when she modeled the dress for him. The strapless bodice dipped in front in what the salesclerk called a sweetheart neckline, to fit snugly around her torso and lift and display the gentle swell of her bosom.

The frothy skirt flared at the waist and floated bewitchingly with every step she took, ending far above her knee to bare a large amount of long, slender leg and thigh.

He swallowed hard, wondering what it would be like to have those satiny legs wrapped around his waist, to slip the bodice of that enticing dress down over the tips of her breasts and—

"Charles?"

Shaking himself back to reality, he mumbled, "What?"

Mari glanced in a mirror. "What do you think? Is it too...daring?"

He strove to keep his voice light. "Daring, yes, but not too much so. No one will be able to keep their eyes from you." Especially him.

"You think Jordan will like it?"

A savage denial ripped through him as he thought of Jordan and his cool hands against her waist, holding her tight in a dance, gazing down at the sweet flesh rising above her bodice. Jordan didn't deserve her, but it wasn't Charles's place to tell her that.

"Yes," he bit out. "Jordan will like it." And if he didn't, no doubt there were many other men who would.

"I'll take it." Mari paid for the two dresses and they left the shop. "Now what?"

They spent the rest of the morning shopping for just the right accessories for her two new dresses, and after lunch Charles persuaded her to get her hair cut and have a facial and a makeover while he waited patiently and watched the whole process.

It was worth the wait to see Mari emerge from the beauty salon with a glow of self-confidence. She looked her best and she obviously knew it, with a bouncy new hairstyle that looked charming and a sup-

ply of new cosmetics that enhanced her natural
beauty.

"What's next?" she asked eagerly.

"It's almost dinnertime. Are you ready to go
home?"

For a moment disappointment flashed across her
face, then it was gone as quickly as it had come.

"What's wrong?" he asked.

"Nothing. It's just…I've been having so much fun.
No one has ever pampered me like this before and I
was just beginning to enjoy it." She gazed at him
with a wistful expression. "I don't want it to end."

He grinned. "Ah, but it's not over yet."

"No?" she asked, with a spark of hope in her
voice.

"I have a surprise waiting for you at home." At
least, he hoped it was waiting…if Kirby hadn't forgotten.

More eagerly now, Mari drove home. When they
reached the house, Charles said, "Go change into
your new blue dress, then come over to Kirby's." He
was tempted to tell her to wear the wine-colored
dress, but he didn't think he could be held responsible
for his actions if she did.

"But I don't want to soil it before I wear it tomorrow night."

"Don't worry. If you do, we'll just buy another
one."

"But what—"

"No questions. Just do it."

He escorted her to her bedroom, then departed to
check on the progress of the preparations.

Mari didn't know what Charles had in mind, but
she followed his instructions anyway. Though the day

had been exhausting, she looked forward to seeing what Charles had in store for her next.

She changed into her new clothes and for once in her life she felt absolutely beautiful. If the right dress, accessories and makeup did this for her, she knew she was doing the right thing in marrying Jordan. With him by her side, she knew she could fit in and become the gracious and charming hostess she'd always wanted to be.

Once she changed, she made her way to Kirby's and knocked on the door. Kirby answered it, looking neat and uncomfortable in a suit, with his wayward hair slicked down and his glasses on straight for a change.

"My, Kirby, don't you look handsome," Mari declared. He did, too, which surprised her. She didn't think she'd ever seen him in anything other than jeans and a T-shirt.

"And you look terrific," Kirby said with an awed look. "You're pretty!"

Mari laughed at the astonishment in his voice, then heard someone clearing their throat on the other side of the door. Suddenly self-conscious, Kirby straightened his tie and intoned in a self-important voice, "How do you do, my dear? I'm Reginald Sloan."

He held out his hand to her and Mari took it, smiling as she figured out what was going on. Charles was giving her this chance to practice her self-assurance before the dinner party.

Playing along, Mari shook his hand, saying, "Mr. Sloan, I'm so happy to meet you. I've been looking forward to this for a long time."

Kirby nodded, then said, "And may I introduce my wife, Myra?"

He drew Charles out from his hiding place behind the door. Somewhere, Charles had found Mari's frilly white apron and had tied it around his waist, then plopped her gardening hat on his head. The large straw brim with its tattered cabbage roses looked hilarious on him, and it was all she could do not to burst into laughter.

He raised his nose in the air to peer down at her and held out two fingers for her to shake, saying in a high-pitched voice, "How do you do?"

She bit her lip to keep from laughing, then managed a creditable handshake and murmured, "Happy to meet you."

Kirby ushered her in and closed the door, then he and Charles stood aside as Kirby gestured down at the floor. "And you know our son, Jordan, of course."

There Buster sat, in the middle of the hallway, looking quite dignified and pleased with himself as he sported a black bow tie around his neck, worn slightly askew. A red rose curled around his feet.

Tears stung her eyes as Mari put her hand to her mouth, not knowing whether to laugh or cry. Buster looked adorable, and they had gone to such trouble— all for her.

Charles picked up the flower and handed it to her with a flourish. "For you."

The tears spilled over and ran down her cheeks as she accepted the rose. In a choked voice, she said, "No one's ever given me flowers before."

Charles looked startled, then he patted her on the arm, saying in a falsetto voice, "Now, dear, no need to cry. We know he's not much, but Jordan will grow on you."

Laughter won over tears and Mari couldn't help but let a chuckle escape.

"That's better, dear," Charles said. "Dinner is served. Shall we?" Pausing to scoop up Buster, he said, "You'll have to excuse Jordan. I'm afraid the cat has his tongue tonight."

Giggling, Mari followed Charles and almost began crying again when she saw the dining room. Kirby's old table was covered with an elegant white tablecloth and gleamed with shining china, silverware and crystal—and a huge bouquet of beautiful red roses.

"Kirby," she said in a choked voice. "I had no idea you had all these lovely place settings...or knew how to arrange them."

Falling out of character for a moment, Kirby confided, "I don't, really. I rented them for the night—and the rental people showed me how to set them up. Does it look all right?"

"It looks perfect." She kissed him on the cheek. "Thank you."

Kirby hunched his shoulder in an embarrassed shrug. "It was Charles's idea."

Mari had no choice but to give Charles a peck on the cheek, too, saying, "Thank you, too."

"Oh, my dear, how sweet," Charles warbled, still in character. "But do let us eat."

Kirby seated her, and Charles produced a large domed serving tray. "You'll have to excuse us, it's the servants' night off." With a flourish, he removed the lid, saying, "I do hope you like Chinese."

A variety of white cartons from her favorite Chinese take-out restaurant were stacked neatly on the tray. Mari laughed. "I love it."

That set the tone for the rest of the evening as

Kirby and Charles became Mr. and Mrs. Sloan and tested her burgeoning confidence with impertinent and outrageous questions about her background. She'd never laughed so much or enjoyed herself quite so thoroughly. She even managed not to spill anything on her new dress.

But finally the evening had to end, and after giving Kirby and Charles each one last hug, she took Buster to bed with her. It had been a marvelous day, and she couldn't remember ever having so much fun before.

Now, if only tomorrow would be the same...

Her self-confidence lasted through the night and into the next day as she and Charles continued to study the books she'd brought home. It didn't begin to waver until she was sitting alone in her bedroom, staring into the mirror. Then all her doubts came rushing back.

The dress and makeup were really only superficial trappings that added a surface gloss over the real Mari. Who was she trying to kid? She was no socialite. She was just plain Marigold Boles.

Still, she dressed as she had the previous night, so as not to disappoint Charles. He had gone to such trouble to make this evening easy for her, and she didn't want to disappoint him.

Charles was still in the living room, reading. She stood in front of him, twisting her hands together nervously. "Well, what do you think?"

Charles looked up from his book and smiled. "You look beautiful, just like last night." His eyes narrowed and he added, "But something's wrong."

"What?" In a panic, Mari mentally checked the entire outfit. What had she forgotten?

"Look at your arms."

Mari looked down. Once more, her traitorous arms had wrapped themselves around her middle.

"You're nervous again."

"I can't help it. This is so important, and I have this awful feeling that something is going to go terribly wrong."

"Your nerves are getting the better of you. Remember last night? You did so well."

"Yes, but that's because I knew you really weren't the Sloans. Just Kirby and Charles." She grinned. "And Buster, of course."

"You're going to do just as well tonight," Charles said with supreme confidence. "Just remember, you're fighting for your future."

She lowered her head to consider what he'd said. Fighting for her future. Yes, fighting for the right to never be lonely again, to finally belong somewhere, to belong *to* someone and have that person belong to her. Charles was right. She could do this.

She raised her chin, surprised to find him standing in front of her, offering her another red rose with a crooked smile. How sweet. Why couldn't Jordan be this nice? She took the rose and inhaled its sweet fragrance. "Thank you," she whispered.

He inclined his head. "You're quite welcome."

They exchanged a look of mutual understanding and affection and a spark of something more kindled in Charles's eyes. Mari took a step toward him, but the doorbell rang, halting her. She hesitated, reluctant to break the mood, but duty called. "That must be my parents. Jordan is picking us all up here."

Charles nodded, his gaze now shuttered.

She answered the door, discouraging the persistent kitten from trying to get outside. She gave her parents a hug, then escorted them into the living room, gesturing with her rose. "Charles, these are my parents, John and Sally Boles. Mom and Dad, this is Charles..." She hesitated for a moment, unsure how much to reveal to them. "Charles...Boles."

Her mother turned to him in delight. "Boles? Are you a relative?"

Hurriedly, Mari interrupted. "He might be. Charles is...related to Black Bart, too. We, uh, learned about the connection, so Charles is staying here to learn more about him."

Charles shot her a startled glance, but Mari knew her freethinking parents wouldn't be worried about the thought of a man living with her. They trusted her, and if she wanted to have a man live with her, that was her business.

"How marvelous," her mother exclaimed. "Did you hear that, dear? Charles is related to Black Bart, too."

"Yes," her father said and shook Charles's hand. "He even has the same first name."

"That's right," her mother exclaimed.

The three of them segued into a discussion of their supposed common ancestor, as Mari watched with a small smile on her face. Her parents were obviously enchanted with Charles and she could tell by the look on his face that he was enjoying their open, honest expressions of delight.

All too soon the doorbell rang. Knowing it was Jordan, Mari interrupted to tell her parents, "Jordan is a bit old-fashioned, so I told him Charles is my cousin. You won't give me away, will you?"

"Of course not," her mother said, but her expression was filled with amused curiosity.

Mari fidgeted with her rose. ''And I forgot to mention this earlier, but his parents are really down on Black Bart because they made their fortune in Wells Fargo. It's causing a little problem with our engagement, so don't mention him to the Sloans, okay?''

Her parents exchanged an odd look and her father said, ''Maybe we should—''

''Please, just promise me.''

Her mother patted her hand. ''I promise, dear.''

''Thank you,'' Mari said in real relief.

The doorbell pealed once again, and Mari went to answer it. ''Jordan, how are you?'' she asked, and presented her lips for a kiss.

Jordan placed a dry peck on her cheek. ''I'm fine. Are you ready?''

''Yes, come in and meet my parents.''

She led him into the living room and couldn't help but notice a small frown crease his brow as he caught sight of Charles. She introduced him to her parents and waited nervously for his reaction.

Her heart sank as his features froze into a polite mask of welcome and his gaze flicked over her parents' clothing. Being a product of the sixties as they were, they still eschewed formal wear and chose to wear more comfortable clothing.

Her willowy mother was dressed formally—for her—in a flowing purple caftan dotted with gold stars, moons and suns. Mari thought she looked beautiful, but it appeared Jordan had a different interpretation.

Her stepfather didn't seem to pass muster, either, though Mari knew he had done his utmost, wearing his best jeans and boots with a white shirt, a navy sport coat and a string bolo tie. He looked a bit self-conscious in his finery, but she was touched that he had taken the trouble to dress up for her.

Jordan's face froze in a mask of disdain, though he hid it quickly and was excruciatingly polite. Mari bristled, but there was nothing she could do or say unless Jordan said something overt. Her parents might be middle-class, but they were fine people and generous to a fault.

Unfortunately she could also tell that her parents, no dummies, had picked up on Jordan's feelings, and they, too, turned polite but distant. Mari turned to Charles, seeking his support.

He just shook his head and gave her a compassionate look. Mari sighed inwardly. The evening wasn't exactly off to an auspicious start.

Jordan glanced down at the rose she still held in her hands. "What's that? I hope it's not for my mother. She's allergic to roses."

Mari felt a blush color her cheeks. "No, it's, uh, for me—from Charles and Kirby."

Before Jordan could say anything more, Charles plucked the flower from her fingers. "I'll put it in water for you so it will be waiting until you get home."

She flashed him a grateful smile then turned to Jordan. "Shall we go?" she asked brightly. Might as well get it over with.

The drive to the Sloans was short, enlivened only by stilted conversation about the weather and other harmless subjects. Mari's heart sank. This was the first time her parents had met Jordan, and she'd wanted them to like each other. She hadn't expected adoration, but it would be nice if her future husband could get along with her parents.

As they drove up to the Sloans' house, Mari gulped. It was big, expensive and practically screamed wealth and privilege— just as she'd expected. Her parents exchanged another odd glance as they exited the car. Their nonverbal sign language had evolved over many years of marriage, and Mari'd never been able to interpret it. Not for the first time, she wished she could. Did that significant look mean they were intimidated, or happy for their daughter, or unimpressed by the ostentatious display of wealth?

She couldn't worry about that now. They approached the front door and something began chasing round and round in her stomach. It couldn't be butterflies—they were too pretty and exotic—these had to be moths. She grimaced. Moths in her stomach— what an appealing thought.

The grimace was still on her face when the door opened. Luckily, a maid and not Mrs. Sloan caught the force of her expression, though Mari hastily wiped it from her face.

At Jordan's murmured instructions, they all silently followed the maid into a spacious living area easily the size of Mari's house, decorated in the latest style. A couple rose from the couch and stood waiting for them to approach. Mr. and Mrs. Sloan, she assumed.

Mrs. Sloan was a tall patrician beauty with pale blond hair. Every hair was rigidly in place and her makeup and attire were flawless, though the expression on her face was forbidding. Jordan had obviously inherited his looks from her.

Mr. Sloan wore a dark charcoal gray suit that must have cost a fortune, and he beamed at them with a false smile.

The moths increased their acrobatics and dread

filled Mari. These did not look like nice people. Jordan introduced them, and his mother held out two fingers.

Mari flashed on an image of Charles doing the same thing the night before in his absurd hat, and she grinned and relaxed. *Thank you, Charles.* Thanks to him, she could probably handle this.

She shook the woman's hand, but didn't miss the distasteful look Mrs. Sloan gave Mari's parents. Mari felt herself bristling again. Who did these people think they were, anyway? Her parents were just as good as the Sloans. Better—they didn't judge people by the clothes they wore or who they were related to.

That defensive feeling sustained her through the predinner drinks and chitchat. The conversation seemed designed to put her parents in as much discomfort as possible as they discussed the various charities Myra Sloan was involved in and the activities of their social set. Somehow Mari managed to respond politely to each sally addressed at her, but she could tell her parents were becoming more and more irritated.

A slight reprieve came when the maid showed them into the dining room, and Mari clutched Jordan's arm. He patted her hand, but his expression was confused and apprehensive. He might not understand what was going on, but she did. The Sloans were uncovering each of the Boleses' weaknesses, subtly showing Jordan how very different their worlds were.

Well, Mari wasn't going to let them get away with it. Remembering what Charles had said, Mari steeled her resolve to fight for her future.

Over the soup, Myra Sloan finished her litany of charities and all-around good deeds and turned to

Mari's mother with a supercilious smile. "And what do you do?"

"Oh, I'm just a housewife," Mom said, her lovely lilting voice suddenly taking on a hillbilly twang. Mari looked at her in surprise as she continued. "I just love to clean and cook for my man, and putter around the garden."

She slapped her husband on the knee and Mr. Sloan winced, though Dad gave her an amused smile.

He had every right to be amused. Putter around the garden, indeed. Mari intervened. "Mother is a master gardener. Her entries always sweep the prizes at the flower shows and she's sought after far and wide for the herbal concoctions she sells."

"How...nice," Myra murmured.

Mom just grinned and waved a negligent hand. "Oh, pshaw."

Pshaw? Her mother *never* said "pshaw."

"That ain't nothin'," she continued. "What you do is real fine. Important like."

Mari didn't know whether to laugh or cry. Her mother was so obviously turning on the dumb routine, making fun of the Sloans in return for the way they were treating her. Strangely enough, the Sloans didn't get it—they really expected the Boleses to behave this way.

"Thank you," Myra murmured and dabbed at her lips with the napkin as the maid served the main course. "And what do you do in your spare time?"

"Oh," Mom declared. "I just *love* to play bingo. Don't I, Johnny Boy?"

"Johnny Boy" just grinned, so Mari decided it was time to intervene. "My mother is putting you on," she explained. To Mari's knowledge, Mom had never played bingo in her life. "She's actively involved in raising funds for AIDS research, working to combat homelessness and teaching adults to read in local literacy programs."

Myra looked taken aback, but it was obvious from her expression that she didn't consider the down-and-dirty work to be worthy of her notice. Heavens, to do what Mari's mother did, you had to get down in the trenches and actually deal with real people.

From there, the evening degenerated. Mari gave up trying to defend her parents. Instead, she watched as they acted like complete hicks. She cast her mother reproachful glances, but Mom ignored them. Evidently she was having too much fun.

Mari retreated into silence, glad at least that the Sloans' scrutiny hadn't turned her way. She didn't think it could get any worse until Reginald Sloan mentioned that his family had made most of their wealth by wisely investing in Wells Fargo.

Mari groaned inwardly when she saw the gleam in her father's eye. He was normally quiet and mild mannered, but she could tell he was becoming very annoyed by the way the Sloans were treating his wife.

"That's a coincidence," he said. "Our family made most of our money by *stealing* from Wells Fargo. You have heard of Black Bart, haven't you?"

Mari almost gasped in horror. What money? Besides, they hadn't made a dime—after Black Bart was caught, he'd returned the stolen cash. That didn't matter, though, not when her parents were on a roll.

Reginald stiffened. "That despicable man?"

Mari's hackles rose. They were talking about *Charles*. Without thinking of the consequences, she burst into the conversation. "He was not despicable.

He was a gentleman—a poet who never harmed anyone. Why, his gun was never even loaded.''

Reginald's expression turned even haughtier. ''That doesn't excuse his perfidy.''

''Perfidy?'' Mari's mother asked in a loud stage whisper that carried to everyone at the table. ''What's perfidy?''

''I don't know,'' her father replied, his accent somehow becoming as bad as hers, ''but I don't think it's good.''

Dad turned to fix Reginald with a beady stare. ''Are you calling my great-great granddaddy dirty names?''

He was making it even worse. It was uncle—not daddy. But Mari kept her mouth shut. If she shouted ''uncle,'' they might take it wrong—and she wasn't about to give up yet.

Jordan apparently felt it time to intervene. ''No, he didn't mean that at all, did you, Father? He meant only that he was still a criminal.''

Dad managed to look even more offended. ''Well, I didn't come here expecting to have my family bad-mouthed. Maybe it's time for us to go.''

Mari's heart sank once again. But she couldn't blame him—she didn't want this evening to continue any more than he did.

''But dessert...'' Jordan protested.

''Perhaps they're right,'' Myra said with a tight smile. She rose from the table, and they all rose with her.

Mari's parents swept toward the door in haughty disdain, as if they'd been mortally offended. The Sloans watched them go with smug satisfaction.

Knowing she would still have to get along with the

Sloans after she married Jordan, Mari tried to contain the damage by pausing to thank her hostess for the evening. Myra's eyes turned cold and condescending, but she accepted Mari's thanks gracefully.

Once outside, Mari expelled a sigh of relief. Thank heavens, the evening was over. Or almost over—they still had to get home.

Jordan showed the Boleses into his car and no one seemed inclined to talk, so the ride was mercifully silent. When they reached her house Mari was all for heading straight for her bed, but it appeared Jordan had other plans. He asked her to wait. She agreed, but escorted her parents to their car first.

Giving them a half amused, half angry glance, she muttered, "I'll talk to *you* later."

Her mother's expression turned soft. "I'm sorry, sweetie, but—"

"It's okay, Mom. I understand." She did, too. Her parents had only retaliated in kind.

"We only want what's best for you, dear. Are you sure Jordan is it?"

Mari felt annoyance surge through her. Why couldn't this be easy? "Yes, Mother," she said firmly. "I'm sure."

Her mother looked doubtful. "Well, if you're positive..." She patted Mari's arm. "I'm sure we'll come to love him. In time."

"Thanks, Mom."

Her parents drove off and Mari walked back to the door where Jordan waited for her.

He greeted her with a frown. "It didn't go well, did it?"

That was the understatement of the century. Irritated, she said, "No, Jordan, it didn't. Your parents were snobbish—"

"*My* parents? What about yours?"

"They weren't snobs."

"No, but they managed to make fun of my parents with their put-on hayseed accents."

She raised her eyebrows, surprised he'd noticed what his parents had missed. "They were only responding to your parents' rudeness."

"Rude? How were they rude?"

She couldn't believe he could see through her parents' deception and not see what was staring him in the face in his own. "They made darned sure they pointed out the difference in their social classes."

"Nonsense," Jordan declared. "You're imagining things. They were only being polite and discussing the things they're familiar with. I can't help it if your parents didn't understand."

Their voices had escalated so that Mari was afraid they'd wake the neighborhood if they continued this discussion any further. Tears stung her eyes. This was their first fight, and she didn't want it to ruin what had been a very comfortable relationship up to now.

She moved closer to Jordan and clutched his lapel, looking up into his eyes. She waited for affection to envelop her, as it did when Charles held her, but there was nothing.

Maybe it was just because they were arguing. "Let's not fight about this, okay?"

Jordan glanced down at her but didn't move. "Why did you defend them? It's not like you to be so...bold."

A flash of annoyance coursed through her, but she suppressed it. "They're my parents, silly," she said in the adoring voice he seemed to like. "What did you expect me to do? Detail all their faults?"

Jordan relaxed. "I guess not."

She cajoled him further. "I just wanted so much for them to like each other. For your sake. For us."

He sighed, as if in relief that the old Mari was back. Squeezing her shoulders, he gave her a kiss on the forehead. "I want that, too. What do you say we have dinner the day after tomorrow—just the two of us?"

Mari smiled. "I'd like that."

Jordan turned to leave, then paused and said, "Don't worry, my folks will come around. I'll talk to them."

Mari's smile froze in place as she murmured, "Good." But Jordan was living in a dream world. No way would they accept her as a daughter-in-law, especially after tonight.

Chapter Seven

Charles and Kirby chatted in Mari's kitchen, both trying to pretend they weren't marking time while waiting for her to get home. After the mock dinner party Charles felt a sort of proprietary interest in the outcome of her evening, and it appeared Kirby felt the same. Even Buster looked worried as he sat in Charles's lap, alert to anything that moved.

At the sound of a car door slamming, Charles and Kirby exchanged glances. Kirby peered out the kitchen window. "It's Mari." He watched for a few minutes, then said, "Her parents are leaving, but she's still talking to Jordan." He let the curtain fall. "I wonder why they're home so early?"

Charles had been wondering that as well. In perfect accord, Charles, Kirby and Buster went to wait in the hallway. Charles knew this was important to her and had to know how the evening had gone. Had they helped her at all?

Struck by a thought, he asked, "Will she invite Jordan in?"

Kirby pondered that for a moment, then shook his head. "I don't think so, not when she's spending so much time talking to him outside."

They heard her at the door and turned toward it with expectant looks. She entered alone and came to a halt when she spotted them, a look of surprise on her face.

Charles stood there awkwardly and cleared his throat. "Uh, how did it go?"

For a moment, Mari did nothing. Then she said, "Oh, it was awful." Her face crumpled and she looked like she was close to tears.

Wordlessly Charles held out his arms and Mari flew into them, sobbing on his shoulder. As he murmured soothing sounds, he caught a glimpse of Kirby who appeared shocked to see Mari in Charles's arms. Had Kirby expected Mari to turn to him? Not wanting to see Kirby hurt, Charles made a small gesture to indicate his bafflement.

Kirby's expression turned thoughtful, then he nodded in apparent understanding and left quietly.

Charles returned his attention to the woman weeping in his arms. What had Jordan done to her? If that bastard had harmed her in any way, he'd have Charles to reckon with. For a moment he felt a murderous rage consume him, then it dissipated, leaving stunned incomprehension in its wake.

He hadn't realized his capacity for anger was so large. Coming on top of the realization that he was Black Bart, it was disturbing—a new part of his personality he wasn't sure he wanted to contend with.

Mari raised her head, and Charles damped down his reaction. There was no time to deal with that now. Mari needed him. "Shall we go into the living room?"

She nodded, so Charles led her to the couch. He seated himself and she curled up next to him, laying her head on his shoulder. It was such a natural gesture that he felt touched and pleased. She was coming to trust him, though Lord knew she had no reason to, especially if she ever caught a glimmer of the lascivious thoughts going on in his mind. "Tell me about it," he urged.

"It was terrible," she reiterated. "Just awful."

"What happened?"

"The Sloans were much worse than we expected." She gave him a watery grin. "You and Kirby were raw amateurs by comparison."

The kitten meowed plaintively at their feet. Charles chuckled. "And Buster, don't forget him." He picked the kitten up and placed him on Mari's lap, where he obviously longed to be. Contented, Buster curled up and purred in satisfaction as she stroked his fur.

"Well, he did a good job of playing Jordan. Like Buster, Jordan pretty much just sat there the whole night."

"He didn't come to your aid?" Charles asked in indignation.

"No, it wasn't like that. The Sloans didn't attack *me*. They were too smart for that. Instead, they made sly little digs at my parents, trying to show them up as beneath them."

"And did they?" Mari's parents were nice people—he didn't want to see them hurt.

Mari gave a watery chuckle. "Not really. Mom and Dad caught on right away to what they were doing. So they gave the Sloans what they were expecting."

"You mean—"

"Mother was the worst. All of a sudden, she started talking with a nasal twang and her table manners were awful. She turned loud and obnoxious, and pretended she didn't understand some of the words Mrs. Sloan was using. Then she bragged about being a simple little housewife—which she isn't—and said she played *bingo* of all things."

Charles could just picture it. Despite himself, he chuckled, then immediately regretted it. "I'm sorry," he apologized. "I had no right—"

"Don't worry about it. It is funny, though it didn't seem so at the time."

He reached out to stroke her cheek. "Was it so terrible?"

She sighed and nuzzled into his hand. "Yeah, it was. What's worse is that Jordan's parents didn't even realize Mom was making fun of them. If they ever find out, I shudder to think what might happen."

"They won't."

"It doesn't matter. They hate me, I can tell." Tears welled up in her eyes again. "They'll never accept me as Jordan's wife."

Charles hated to see her cry. "The more fools they," he declared and gathered Mari in his arms. He'd been waiting for an excuse to do so ever since the last time they'd sat entwined on this couch. She felt so right nestled against his heart, as if she belonged there. Jordan didn't appreciate her, didn't deserve her.

Charles thought about telling her that, but he knew she wouldn't believe it. "It'll be all right," he murmured into her sweet-smelling hair.

"How?"

Charles pulled back to gaze into her tearstained face. Her eyes were wide and bright and her full, sensuous lips trembled. It struck him to the heart to see her so unhappy.

He wiped away a tear with his thumb and brushed a few errant strands of hair out of her face. "Perhaps Jordan will disregard his parents' wishes," he murmured.

"You think he might?" she asked, hope rising in her voice.

"How can he not?" Charles murmured. He stroked her cheek, then buried his fingers in the soft strands of hair at her neck. He knew it was wrong, but he couldn't help himself. She was so enchanting and desirable. He lowered his face to hers, saying, "You're so kind, so gentle, so beautiful." He murmured the last words on a breath, as their lips remained only a kiss away.

Pleasure lit her face as Mari stared into his eyes and whispered, "Beautiful?"

"Ravishing," he affirmed and moved that small distance to capture her lips with his. Their lips clung together for an endless moment and Charles felt a small pang of remorse. He was a married man...and he was kissing an engaged woman. But none of that mattered now. He couldn't feel guilty about a wife he couldn't even remember.

Mari's tentative response made Charles's heart well up in his chest as a shaft of excitement and pure need stabbed through him. Unable to stop himself, Charles claimed her lips for another kiss, slowly, so as not to frighten her. Mari inhaled sharply and wound her arms about his neck, returning his embrace. Her unexpected fervor caught him off guard and served to fuel his ardor even more. He pressed her to him, molding her body against his on the narrow confines of the sofa.

She opened her mouth, inviting him in. He accepted the invitation, tasting the sweetness of her mouth, thrilling at the tentative exploration of her tongue. Wanting her nearer, as close as possible, he pressed her more firmly against his body.

A muffled yowl split the silence and Charles felt a flurry of activity around his abdomen. Surprised, he drew back, and Buster shot out of the space between them. The kitten landed awkwardly on the floor, then righted himself, shook himself off, and sauntered away with tail-swinging dignity, casting an indignant glance over his shoulder.

Mari chuckled and Charles laughed along with her. She glanced at him shyly and Charles pulled away, the mood broken. "I'm sorry, Mari, I had no right—"

"It's okay. I—I was as much to blame as you." Her gaze slid away from his. "You're very good at...providing comfort."

It had gone far beyond comfort, more into the realm of desire and need, but Charles didn't correct her. Let her keep her illusions for now. He cleared his throat and smoothed the soft skin on her cheek. "As I was saying, you're so lovely no man would be able to resist you for long."

She blushed and gazed up at him with something that looked a great deal like longing in her eyes. "You really think so?"

"Yes, I do," he whispered, adding, "not even Jordan." She stiffened, but he pressed the point. "Are you sure Jordan is the man for you?"

Mari pulled away. "Why does everyone keep asking me that? Of course I'm sure."

Charles remained silent, knowing anything he said now would be wrong.

Mari straightened her mussed clothing and moved

to put some distance between them. "No matter what anyone says, I *will* marry Jordan. And I *will* make the Sloans accept me...whether they like it or not." She flounced off the sofa and headed for her bedroom. Over her shoulder, she tossed, "And *you're* going to help me do it."

Charles watched her leave with regret. Yes, he'd still help her by trying to become a model citizen, but after tonight he wasn't sure how well it was going to work. How could she reform him when he couldn't even keep his hands off her?

SURPRISINGLY, MARI SLEPT well. She'd expected to toss and turn all night, but the variety of emotions surging through her had left her so exhausted she'd fallen asleep immediately.

With morning came a new perspective. As she took a shower and dressed, she realized Charles was right. She had to fight for what she believed in. This time she wasn't going to be left on the outside looking in. This time she was going to belong, even if she had to force the Sloans to accept her.

A pang of guilt assailed her. Was it right to shove herself into their family this way? If she really loved Jordan, it would be understandable. But she didn't...yet. Did he deserve to marry someone who wasn't in love with him?

Mari thought it over for a few minutes, then decided he did. Jordan was a misfit, too. If he didn't marry her, he might not find anyone else who understood the pain of not belonging. Besides, she did feel affection for him. In time, she was certain it would turn into love.

The problem lay in making sure Jordan stayed in

love with her. After the missed tennis date and that
fiasco of a dinner party, he had seemed very annoyed.
She'd never seen this side of him before, but she was
sure it was just a stress-induced reaction to the situation. After she reformed Charles and sent him back
in time, there would be no more stress, and she and
Jordan could continue with their same comfortable
relationship.

She paused. A comfortable relationship? Would
that be enough?

It would have to be. It was the only option, after
all. Jordan was the first man who'd paid any attention
to her in years. She couldn't lose him and take the
chance that there might be someone out there more
exciting, more interesting…more like Charles.

Now where had that thought come from? A wistful
longing swept through her as she remembered the previous night…and Charles's kisses. Jordan had never
made her feel like *that*—as if she were so beautiful
and desirable that he couldn't keep his hands off
her…as if she were a cherished piece of exquisite
china…as if she mattered.

Mari sighed. If only Charles could stay. Maybe…

She shook her head. No. That wouldn't happen. He
had to leave, and she had to stay here and marry Jordan. She nodded decisively, trying to ignore the sinking feeling in her stomach. She had to take the long
view and do what was right for her future happiness,
not live for the moment, no matter how much she
longed to do so.

Mari went in search of Charles, steeling herself
against his charm. She found him in the kitchen as
expected, drinking coffee and talking to Kirby about

more time experiments with—of all things—a potted begonia sitting between them.

They looked so cozy and comfortable as they chatted and played with Buster that she couldn't help a tremulous smile. This is what she wanted—a real family to share good times and bad. But these guys, wonderful as they were, didn't belong to her, and she refused to settle for second best. She wanted the works—a husband, a home and lots of children and animals running around.

For that, she needed Jordan—and Charles was the key. She entered the kitchen and said in a cheery voice, "So, Charles, are you ready to do some more research today?"

He looked up in surprise, a bit of wariness on his face. "Yes, of course."

"Then let's go to Phoenix and see if we can find those book titles I found on the Internet." He rose, and she added, "It's a long drive and it might take a while to find what we want, so we'll probably spend the night there. You might want to bring a change of clothes."

Charles nodded and went off to his room, presumably to do as she suggested. Kirby stared at her with an odd expression, almost as if he suspected there was something going on—as if he thought she was doing this just to be alone with Charles.

Mari felt her face flame despite herself. She hadn't thought of that at all. Defensively she said, "Will you take care of Buster for me while I'm gone? Feed him?"

Kirby glanced down at the kitten. "Sure. I guess. If I remember."

"Don't worry, I'll make sure you remember—I'll

put an automatic reminder on your computer. You won't be able to miss it." She started to head for the door but paused as she remembered the topic of his conversation with Charles. "But you are *not* to use Buster in any experiments—especially not time experiments. Do you understand me?"

Kirby looked offended. "Of course. Trust me, I wouldn't do that after you asked me not to."

"Then what experiments were you and Charles talking about?"

"I still plan to conduct experiments on the time field, but not with Buster."

"Oh? What unsuspecting creature have you planned to terrify now?" she asked in resignation, wondering who she'd have to rescue this time.

"Not a creature," Kirby explained. "That." He nodded toward the kitchen table.

"The begonia?"

"Right." Shooting her a resentful glance, he said, "I realize you object to using animals, so this will do just fine. It's animate, too."

Time-traveling begonias? What would he think of next? Shaking her head, she went to schedule his computer so he wouldn't forget to feed and water Buster.

When she finished, she found Charles furtively shoving something Kirby had given him in his back pocket.

"Ready to go?" she asked, wondering what they were up to.

"Yes, of course."

He acted as though nothing had happened, so Mari let it drop, occupied as she was with trying to prevent Buster from making another escape attempt.

They headed out, down the freeway on the two-and-a-half-hour drive to Phoenix. Charles seemed quite used to the car now and was even able to relax. He spent most of his time gazing at the beautiful scenery of Sedona and Oak Creek Canyon, then appeared disappointed when the red mountains and lush greenery faded to the pale green and brown of typical Arizona desert and scrub brush.

Finally he spoke. "There are so few people here."

"On the road, you mean? Well, it's a weekday. It gets busier on the weekends."

"No, I mean towns. There are so few buildings, communities."

"You thought the future would be nothing but one big city or something?"

He hesitated. "I suppose."

"Well, it's not like that. In fact, I'm beginning to think the overpopulation problem predicted in the seventies was a gross exaggeration. There's more open space right here in Arizona than anyone could dream of."

"There are only a few cities, then?"

"No, I wouldn't say that. There are some large cities in the state and quite a few small towns, but most of Arizona is arid. It's hard to live on the land or farm without ready access to water, so most people don't bother. They live in the cities instead."

"And is Phoenix large or small?"

She chuckled. "Large. Very large. That's why we're going there. Because of its size, it has a lot of libraries that should have what we're looking for."

Charles slanted her an assessing glance, as if he wanted to say something but wasn't sure how.

"What does that look mean?" she asked.

He hesitated, then asked, "Are you still set on marrying Jordan?"

"Yes, of course," she said with more vehemence than the situation warranted.

"I thought after last night..."

"After last night, what?"

"I thought perhaps you might have...changed your mind. It seems a formidable task, to get his parents to accept you."

"Maybe," she conceded. "But you convinced me I have to fight for what I want, for what I believe in. And that's Jordan."

"And how does he feel about this?"

"Oh, he thinks he'll be able to bring his parents around."

Charles cast her a speculative look. "You don't believe it, though."

"That's where you come in. If we can prevent you from becoming Black Bart, Jordan and I won't have all this...stress in our relationship and everything will be just fine."

"Stress? Do you want to tell me about it?" he asked softly.

Surprisingly she did. She had to talk to someone. "He...he's not very happy with me right now."

"Why not?"

"I think he's a little angry at me for standing up for my parents when his were so rude."

"Angry? How so?"

She shrugged. "I don't know. As if...as if he's disappointed in me or something."

"How could he be angry with you for someone else's actions?"

That was one reason she liked Charles—he stuck up for her. "I guess because I wasn't sorry enough."

Charles's eyebrows rose at that and he opened his mouth to speak, then paused, apparently rethinking what he had to say. Carefully he said, "I'm certain once he thinks it over he'll realize you're not to blame. He'll come around."

"Maybe. I'm not so sure. I'm sure I'll blow it."

"Blow it?"

"Mess it up," she explained. "We have a date tomorrow night, and I'll probably be a total klutz. Then he'll see just how much of an idiot I really am."

"That's not going to happen."

She chuckled without humor. "That's what you think. Knowing me, it's inevitable—believe me."

"We'll see," Charles said enigmatically. "Looks like it's time for another lesson."

He didn't offer an explanation, so Mari didn't ask for one. They rode for a few miles in silence, until she noticed a frown creasing Charles's brow. "What's wrong?" she asked.

"When you spoke of last evening, it made me think."

"Think about what?"

"About me. About my reactions to you and your fiancé."

It was obvious he didn't like Jordan, but there had to be more to it than that. "What reactions?"

He frowned. "I'm not certain this is something I should be discussing with you."

"Why not? I've been dumping my troubles on you ever since we met. Why don't you return the favor and let *me* feel self-righteous for a change?"

He chuckled. "All right. When you...fled into my arms, I feared Jordan had hurt you—"

"He didn't," Mari assured him.

"I know that...now, but I didn't at the time."

"So what happened to upset you?"

"Your distress kindled a rage in my heart, a black anger." He cast her a sidelong glance, as if wondering how she was taking his story. "I believe if Jordan had been present at that moment, I would have throttled him."

"And what's wrong with that?" Mari demanded. "It sounds like a perfectly normal reaction to me, for someone who cares about another person." In fact, she found it rather sweet.

"You don't understand. I didn't know I had this sort of violence in my being. It disturbs me greatly."

Suddenly understanding, she patted his hand. "A brief flash of anger doesn't mean you're a murdering psychopath, for heaven's sake. And don't worry—history shows Black Bart wasn't, either."

It didn't seem to help. He still sat there with a morose look on his face. Shaking his head, he said, "I thought I was beginning to know myself, to understand what sort of person I am."

He paused, then continued. "I thought I was beginning to believe Black Bart wasn't such a bad sort after all—"

"He wasn't," Mari assured him. "You aren't."

Charles continued as if she hadn't interrupted. "But after learning my proclivity for violence and debauchery, I am appalled."

"Debauchery? What debauchery?"

His mouth set in a grim line, Charles said, "I'm speaking of the way I treated you."

"Oh, is that all? Don't worry about it. It was just a kiss. I didn't mind." Didn't mind? Hell, she'd enjoyed it...a lot.

"Perhaps not, but where is my honor? I kissed you last night, kissed you even though I knew you were engaged to another man—"

"But—"

"Even though I am a married man, with a wife and children of my own. The fact that I don't remember them is no excuse."

He had her there. The first was her fault as much as his, but his second argument was very persuasive. He did have a wife and children back in time, and it would do no good to deny it.

Charles nodded darkly. "I see by your silence that you agree with me."

Yes, but she couldn't leave him feeling so miserable. "Charles—"

"Whatever you have to say can't take away the simple truth that I am who I am. I am Black Bart...and with this evidence, it appears my heart is blacker than even I feared."

Chapter Eight

The rest of the ride passed in silence as Charles contemplated the elements that made up the person known as Black Bart. It was depressing to realize how his personality traits, slowly being revealed one by one, were beginning to shape the identity and soul of a despised outlaw.

A black cloud settled over him. This journey would lead them into ever more revelations about his life and times as Black Bart. Inevitably he feared the recollections would erode his memory loss until he remembered everything.

Was he ready for that? Could he handle it when it did happen? What if Black Bart was so strong his essence overcame the Charles of here and now, causing Charles to lose all the wisdom he'd gained so far?

Charles shook his head. He couldn't think about that now. He'd just have to guard against Black Bart, follow Mari's plan and hope for the best. He sat up straighter. They were approaching the city, judging by the signs of increased habitation.

"The outskirts of Phoenix," Mari said, confirming his surmise.

Another forty minutes and they were downtown at

the main library branch. Three libraries and six books later, they had what Mari thought they would need.

In the car once more, she turned to him and said, "It's five o'clock. Shall we find a hotel for the evening and grab some dinner? I'm too bushed to drive back."

"That sounds fine with me. Except we won't 'grab' dinner. I have precise instructions from Kirby on where to take you."

Mari's eyebrows rose. "You have instructions from *Kirby*?"

"Yes. He said he's been working you too hard and he wants you to have fun, so he gave me enough money to take you to the...Tortilla Tango, I believe he called it." Charles disliked taking money from Kirby, but he had no choice. All of Charles's belongings, including cash, had been left behind in the past.

"Why, how nice of him. I've been wanting to go there ever since it opened a couple of months ago."

"Why is that?"

"It's supposed to have the best Mexican food in town, with atmosphere up the wazoo, and best of all, dancing."

She sounded so excited Charles couldn't help but smile, though he spared a moment to wonder what the devil a wazoo could be. "We'll go there, then."

"Wonderful."

They found the hotel Kirby had recommended on the outskirts of town and pulled into the parking lot. They registered, getting adjoining rooms. Mari opened the door between the rooms and hung up her clothes, calling out, "The Tortilla Tango is kind of snazzy. Did you bring something nice to change into?"

Charles peered through the open door. "Yes. Kirby warned me about that. I brought the sports jacket, with the shirt and slacks you picked out for me."

"And a tie?"

"No." He'd deliberately left it behind.

She stopped in her unpacking to gaze at him in disappointment. "No tie? But they won't let you in without one."

"How absurd. What purpose does it serve, save as a neck-strangling device and a nod to fashion?"

"It *serves* to get you inside the restaurant." She frowned. "Oh, well, it was a nice idea anyway. We'll go somewhere else."

Her disappointment was palpable. "Nonsense. If all I lack is a tie, surely we can purchase one somewhere." If that's what it took to make Mari happy, then that's what he'd do, regardless of how uncomfortable it made him.

Mari beamed. "Are you sure?"

"Yes, of course."

"All right, then let's hit the mall and find you a tie."

The mall was a fascinating place, full of shops with wondrous merchandise. Mari didn't allow him to dawdle, however, as she pulled him into a men's clothing store.

Once again, she lost her confidence in front of a strange salesclerk and tried to fade into the background, wrapping her arms around her waist and jostling a table as she backed into it. Charles sighed. He was going to have to break her of that habit.

At least this time he knew what they were looking for. He dealt with the salesclerk himself, asking to see a selection of ties. The man presented them with a bewildering array of colors and patterns, saying, "Would you like something conservative or a little loony?"

"Loony?" Charles repeated. He'd never heard that term applied to male attire before.

"You know," the man said. "Like *Looney Tunes.* Cartoons?" He held up a tie with a stylized drawing of a yellow bird. "Here's Tweety—or we have Daffy, Bugs, Porky, you name it."

Charles stared at him in bewilderment. Each individual word made sense on its own, but taken as a whole the meaning was obscure to say the least. What foreign tongue was this? Charles silently appealed to Mari for a translation.

She chuckled and lost some of her reserve as she came to his rescue. "I think we'd better go with something conservative."

With obvious disappointment, the clerk led them to another rack.

Not knowing what to look for, Charles turned to Mari and said, "You choose."

Mari sorted through the ties until she found a couple she liked and presented them to him for his final selection. He chose one at random, not really caring what he wore.

They paid for it, then Charles asked, "Could you show me how to wear it, please?"

The man cast him a puzzled look and muttered, "Where are you from, anyway?"

Charles wasn't sure if he was supposed to hear that or not, but irritated by the man's attitude, he answered nonetheless. "I'm from another time."

"Zone," Mari added quickly. "Another time zone. You know how it is. Jet lag?"

The man nodded in understanding and began to remove the tie from the bag.

"It's okay," Mari added. "Don't bother. I'll show him how to do it."

She grabbed the bag and Charles's arm and hurried them both out of the store. "Why did you say *that*?" she whispered in a fierce tone.

"The man had me at a loss. I didn't know what else to say."

Mari just rolled her eyes. "Yeah, right. You didn't know what else to say, so you told him you were a time traveler."

Exasperated, Charles said, "I just wanted to know if he could understand me. I couldn't understand a word *he* was saying."

Mari stared at him for a moment, then one corner of her mouth quirked upward. A smile followed, then a hearty chuckle. "I can see why you'd think so." She laughed harder. "You should have seen your face when he started talking about Tweety."

Her merriment was contagious and Charles found himself smiling. "I imagine I looked bewildered."

"Totally clueless," she confirmed. "You've been adapting so well, I sometimes forget how different things must appear to you."

"Please, tell me, what is a Tweety?"

"Tweety and those other characters he mentioned are cartoons." When he shook his head, she said, "Caricatures?"

"Caricatures of what?"

"Well, Tweety is a caricature of a bird. They're animated to tell a story in what's called a cartoon...on television."

He wasn't certain he understood her explanation. "Television?"

She patted him on the arm. "Never mind. That's one evil I don't plan to introduce you to. Let's skip the cartoon explanation, okay? It's not something you'll need to know in the nineteenth century."

"All right." He had the distinct impression he wouldn't understand further clarification anyway. "Shall we go back to the hotel to change for dinner?"

They did so, and Charles refused to give up his boots, vest, and hat, though he did put on the shirt, slacks and jacket as Mari requested. The tie baffled him, though. He knocked on the adjoining door to get Mari's assistance with it.

She smiled and draped it around his neck. "Why don't you know how to tie one of these?" Before he could say anything, she answered for him. "Oh, you wore cravats then, didn't you? I imagine they were tied differently."

"I imagine so." He couldn't remember wearing either a tie or a cravat, but it wouldn't disturb him if he never learned how to wear one of these monstrosities.

Mari bit her lip as she stared at the tie. "I...think I remember how to do this. I learned how to do it for Kirby."

As she performed complicated passes with the cloth, Charles stared down at her. She looked so bright and sunny in her sleeveless yellow dress with its full, short skirt—like a touch of springtime. She stood close, near enough for him to inhale the fresh fragrance of her hair. It, too, smelled of flowers in springtime.

It felt so intimate, like something a wife would do

for her husband. A bolt of longing pierced him as he imagined what it would be like to have this woman as his mate. He quickly banished the thought and hardened his resolve. That could never be—she belonged to Jordan. Besides, Charles was a rogue. A reluctant one, yes, but a rogue nonetheless. And Mari deserved better.

Mari gave his tie one last tug and said, "That ought to do it." She remained where she was, her hands and forearms warm upon his lapels, smiling up at him.

Before his resolve could weaken, Charles jerked away from her sweet temptation. "Wait here," he said. "I'll return shortly."

He closed the door in her bewildered face and hurried downstairs to the flower shop he'd seen earlier. The salesclerk assisted him with his purchase and Charles hurried back upstairs. Straightening his tie, he knocked on Mari's door.

When she opened it with a puzzled expression, he swept off his hat and let his voice take on the nasal tones Jordan affected, saying, "You look lovely this evening, my dear. And here is but a small embellishment to add even more to your beauty." He handed her a single red rosebud corsage, then with a grin, he presented her with the bouquet he'd hidden behind his back.

Mari gazed down at the rosebud, her lower lip trembling. She touched it with gentle fingers. "How pretty." Tears filled her eyes and she blinked rapidly.

"Is something amiss?"

"No. It's just...I've never had a corsage, either." She gestured helplessly at the enormous bouquet. "Between that and these beautiful roses, I don't know what to say. Thank you."

Though he was annoyed at Jordan for not giving such a small courtesy to his fiancée, Charles also experienced a glow of satisfaction that he was able to make up for the lack.

They moved inside the room and she put the bouquet in water, then fumbled with the rosebud and its pin.

"Here, let me help you," Charles offered. He pinned the bud to her bodice, taking his time as his fingers lingered over her warm skin and he inhaled her fresh scent once more. He didn't know why he tortured himself so, but the sensations were intoxicating.

Mari leaned down to inhale the sweet aroma of the corsage, and looked up at him once more, unshed tears sparkling in her eyes as she said, "Thank you."

Her expression was filled with tender gratitude...and something more. Charles was tempted to pursue that, but hesitated to take advantage of her vulnerability. Drawing himself up to look down his nose at her, he performed his Jordan imitation again. "Well, then, as your fiancé, it appears I shall have to give you flowers more often."

She glanced up. "My fiancé?" Her gaze was puzzled for a moment, then her brow cleared. "Oh, I see. We're practicing again—for my date tomorrow night?"

Charles sniffed, still staring down his nose. "I don't know what you're talking about." Dropping his pose, he leaned down to whisper confidingly. "Shh. He," he said, jerking his thumb over his shoulder, "thinks he's Jordan. Don't disabuse of the notion or he might turn...violent."

Mari chuckled, a delightful little gurgle. "Okay," she whispered back. "I'll be careful."

They both straightened, and Charles offered her his arm. "Shall we go, then?"

"That sounds wonderful."

She took her keys out of her purse, but Charles forestalled her. "There will be no need for you to drive. I'll handle it."

"You? Since when did you learn how to drive?"

Still in character, Charles said, "Why, Mari, I'm surprised at you. Everyone knows how to drive. But tonight, it won't be necessary."

Ignoring her puzzled look, he escorted her downstairs to the lobby and noted with relief that Kirby had followed through as promised. Charles gestured toward the horse-drawn conveyance, saying, "Madame, your carriage awaits."

The driver held the door open for her, but Mari paused, her eyes wide in astonishment as she clutched her hands to her chest. "Oh, Charles," she breathed. "How romantic."

Inwardly Charles exulted at being able to provide her with such a nice surprise, but outwardly he stiffened. "Charles? Who is Charles? I'm Jordan."

Then, becoming himself again, he whispered, "This was Kirby's idea, too," and helped her into the vehicle.

"Kirby? I don't believe it," she said in a whisper.

Delighted that she was playing along, Charles whispered back, "I asked him how to hire a carriage, and he made the arrangements."

"Now that I believe." Her eyes sparkled as she gazed around the interior. Raising her voice to a normal level as the driver set the vehicle in motion, she said, "This is wonderful...Jordan. What have I done to deserve this?"

Charles shunted aside his instinctive gallant response and tried to determine how her fiancé would respond. Drawing on his experience with the sort of man he knew Jordan to be, and on the little Mari had told him of their disagreement, Charles said, "After that fiasco of a dinner party, I thought I'd show you how our sort lives."

She blinked at him in astonishment. "*Your* sort?" she asked in foreboding tones.

Becoming himself again, Charles said, "The man certainly thinks a lot of himself, doesn't he?" Then louder, "Yes. After all, when you marry me, you'll be living in a very different social sphere. You need to learn how to behave, to belong."

Mari gazed at him thoughtfully, then obviously decided to play along. "And what is it you think I need to learn?"

Charles gave her a condescending pat on the hand, just as Jordan undoubtedly would at this point. "Perhaps a little discretion might not come amiss."

"Discretion?"

"Yes. No doubt you love your parents—"

"No doubt," she said in an uncompromising tone.

"But perhaps you might want to drop a hint in their ear, that they aren't quite up to snuff...?"

"Charles!"

"No, Jordan," he corrected her.

She glared at him. "Do you really think Jordan would say that?"

Charles gave her a compassionate look and dropped the pretense. "Wouldn't he?"

Mari's expression was full of doubt. "I don't

know. Maybe you're right.'' She frowned. ''I don't think I want to deal with that now. Could you…just be Charles?''

Elation surged within him. She preferred him to Jordan? ''Are you sure you don't want to play this out, so you'll know what to say?''

She grimaced. ''No, thanks. Once will be enough. I don't want to go through that twice. Besides, it's not necessary. I've been on dates with Jordan before.''

''But have you been on one quite so important? One where your future is at stake?''

''Well, no, except for the dinner party.''

''And remember how that turned out.''

''True,'' Mari said. ''But even then, your practice was nothing like the real thing. You and Kirby made it fun, even when you were saying horrible things about me as Mrs. Sloan. You made me laugh. The dinner party was nothing like that—I could've used you there.''

''Used me?''

''Yes. I know you believe you're instilling self-confidence in me, but the only time it works is when you're around. When you're with me, I feel I can take on the world. When you're not, I revert back to my old klutzy self.''

No one had ever said anything quite so nice to him before. ''Well, I'll just accompany you on all your outings with Jordan, then, to give you the confidence you need.'' He grinned. ''But it might get a little sticky once you're married.''

She giggled. ''It might. I really do wish you could go with us tomorrow. I'd feel a whole lot better knowing there was someone on my side there.''

So she didn't consider Jordan to be on her side? Charles wondered if she knew how telling that statement was. "I would, but I think Jordan might object."

"Oh, he would." She paused. "Charles, why *don't* you come along? If I at least know you're in the same restaurant, I might have enough confidence to get through this without screwing up."

Come along on her assignation and watch while Jordan made love to her? He didn't think he would be able to stomach it. "I don't think—"

"The Tortilla Tango," the driver said. They'd been so caught up in their conversation, they hadn't even noticed the carriage had come to a stop.

Grateful to the driver for his interruption, Charles escorted Mari out of the vehicle and into the restaurant, murmuring, "We'll speak of that later."

They entered the restaurant and Charles was immediately impressed. The subdued lighting, lush greenery and thick carpets, combined with the tasteful burgundy-and-gold color scheme, lent the establishment an intimate air. As the waiter led them to their table, the clink of silverware and hushed conversation with the occasional sound of laughter didn't detract from that air of intimacy. Rather, it enhanced it.

The waiter seated them at a secluded table near the dance floor and presented them with menus, asking them what they would like to drink.

"Shall we start with champagne?" Charles asked.

"With Mexican food? I don't think so. Why don't we have...frozen margaritas?"

Not wanting to appear ignorant in front of the waiter, Charles agreed. When the waiter left, he leaned over and whispered, "What are margaritas?"

Her eyes sparkling with mischief, Mari asked, "Have you ever eaten Mexican food, drunk tequila?"

The words didn't strike a chord. "I don't know. I don't remember, anyway."

"Then your taste buds are in for a treat. If you liked pizza, you're gonna love this."

She was right. The unusual mixture of the tangy drink, the cold, slushy ice and the salt on the rim of the glass was marvelous. That, combined with the tortilla chips and wonderfully spicy salsa, filled his senses with gustatory delight.

And that was only the beginning. At Mari's urging, he ordered the combination plate. With each dish he tried, old familiar flavors melded with new tastes to burst onto his tongue, providing an adventurous and delightful exploration of his senses.

Mari seemed more interested in his reaction than with her own dinner, so Charles exaggerated his delight for her, closing his eyes in ecstasy and sighing in repletion.

When they were finally finished and every bite of his dinner was gone, Mari chuckled. "I take it you like Mexican food?"

"It was marvelous, an epicurean masterpiece." He glared at his plate. "But I fear I ate too much."

The band started playing and he looked around in pleasure. "How fortuitous. Shall we dance?" He tried to tell himself the exercise would help him digest the large meal he'd just consumed, but he knew it was just an excuse to hold Mari in his arms.

Mari glanced at him in surprise. "Do you know how?"

Did he? A few couples had drifted onto the floor and Charles watched them for a moment as they swayed to the soft music. "I'm not certain, but I believe I can manage it."

Mari smiled. "Well, I'm game if you are."

Dancing came naturally to him, as if he'd done it many times before. Charles didn't bother thinking about it, he just enjoyed the feel of Mari in his arms as they moved to the rhythm of the music.

The margaritas and the Mexican food had opened one of his senses to new experiences, which seemed to have enhanced the others as well. He immersed himself in the sensations—the soft strains of the band, Mari's sweet, fresh fragrance and the intoxicating feel of her in his arms.

As they glided about the floor in an easy rhythm, Charles marveled at how well he and Mari fit together, as if they were made for each other. There was no awkwardness in their movement. It was as if they had been dancing together for years.

They swayed together in silence, in perfect harmony, as Charles dreamed of what it would really be like to be Jordan, to have this wonderful woman as his own. He decided to forget about Black Bart, forget about all the things he was said to have done and just be himself—Mari's Charles.

The seduction of his senses took their toll, and he soon found himself with the inevitable male reaction. As close as they were, it wasn't surprising that Mari felt it, too. He knew the exact moment when realization of his desire impinged on her awareness.

She stiffened as if in surprise and drew away for a moment, then relaxed her hips against his and tightened her embrace. Her simple, trusting movement caught him unaware and a surge of desire rushed through him, almost obliterating all coherent thought.

The band chose that moment to take a break and Charles resolutely untangled himself from Mari's arms to save his sanity, not to mention his control. "It's getting late," he said softly. "Shall we leave?"

Mari gazed up at him with a misty-eyed smile, full of the sensual promise he'd felt in her arms, and nodded.

Charles gulped and hurriedly paid the bill, then left the restaurant to find their driver waiting for them.

Sinking back into the luxury of the carriage with Mari by his side, Charles didn't know what to say, to do. He didn't want this magical night to end, so he placed his arm around Mari's shoulders and drew her close.

She sighed and snuggled into him for the duration of the moonlit ride, her warm, soft body a burning temptation. His desire had not abated and he wanted nothing more than to take her into his arms, peel that yellow dress away from her body and feel the soft weight of her naked breasts in his hands. But he kept himself rigidly in control, not daring to frighten her and lose even this small comfort.

When they reached the hotel, he paid the driver and escorted Mari back to her room. "Come in," she coaxed.

"I don't think—"

"You can get to your room through mine."

Wary of spending any more time near her, yet unable to deny her anything, Charles allowed her to lead him inside the privacy of her room.

She fingered his lapels and gazed up into his eyes. "Thank you, Charles. This has been the most wonderful night of my life."

''And mine,'' Charles whispered, not trusting himself to say more.

Her hands slid up to caress the back of his neck and she raised her face to his. Charles groaned, but didn't give in to temptation. He must subdue the rogue.

''Kiss me, Charles.''

''I shouldn't,'' he ground out.

''It's all right,'' she assured him, nestling her hips against his. ''I'm asking you to.''

''But Jordan—''

''Jordan isn't here. You are.''

He felt his resolve weaken as she dropped small kisses on his jaw. ''We shouldn't,'' he protested. ''There's no future in it.''

''I know,'' Mari whispered. ''But you make me feel as no man ever has before. As no man will again. In a week or so, you'll be gone and all I will have are memories...and Jordan. Help me make beautiful memories,'' she pleaded.

Unable to resist her logic or her seduction, Charles gave in and covered her mouth with his, plunging his tongue deep within her willing mouth. Mari met him thrust for thrust and his desire escalated until he was almost panting with the agony of the unfulfilled.

He raised his head to try and control his ragged breathing and Mari, her face flushed with passion, gazed back at him. He tried to compose himself. Inanely he said, ''We're crushing your corsage. Here, let me remove it for you.''

With shaking hands, he struggled to remove the flower, but the simple act baffled him. He finally succeeded in extricating the small pin from her dress, and his knuckles grazed an out-thrust breast.

Mari inhaled sharply and Charles tossed the corsage onto a nearby table, then experimentally ran the back of his fingers over the taut bud visible through the fabric of her dress.

"Yes," Mari breathed. "Don't stop."

He didn't want to, couldn't. Shakily he unfastened the buttons on the front of her dress until he was able to peel back the fabric and expose one perfect breast to his view. He flicked his tongue over the rosy bud of her nipple and Mari moaned in response, clutching him to her.

That was all the encouragement he needed as Charles ran his tongue around the aureole, then took her fully into his mouth. As he suckled her breast, Mari's hands roamed his body, coming to rest on the hard length between his legs.

At her touch, he almost exploded then and there, and the shock rocked him back to the present. Though his mind was muzzy with desire, he still knew this was wrong. He could go no further.

It was the hardest thing he'd ever done in his life, but Charles raised his head from her breast and pulled her hand away from his loins.

With passion-swollen lips, Mari said, "What's the matter?"

Tenderly replacing the fabric over her breast, Charles said, "We mustn't." Softly he added, "This is not a memory you want to make—not when you plan to marry Jordan someday."

"But—" Mari broke off, sighing. "I guess you're right."

"I know I am." He gave her one last kiss, a chaste one upon her brow. Mari stood there, seductively rumpled by their love play, making him ache with longing. Before he could lose his newfound resolve, he headed toward his own room.

He knew he was right—but why did being right have to be so painful?

Chapter Nine

After fighting with the bedclothes and visions of Mari sleeping next door, Charles estimated he had slept perhaps two hours the whole night. He refused to feel sorry for himself, though. It was all his fault for desiring forbidden pleasures.

Breakfast with Mari was a trifle awkward. No doubt she, too, was remembering the feel of his mouth on her breast, her hand against his straining trousers. When she blushed and knocked over her juice, he was certain of it.

Mild regret filled him. He hadn't meant to make her more uncomfortable, but the rogue in him had taken over. Had he lost all the ground he'd gained?

After breakfast, when they headed back to Sedona, he set aside his own embarrassment and tried to put her at ease. "Did you sleep well last night?"

She averted her eyes. "Yes, of course. Why wouldn't I?"

Charles cursed himself. He'd just made the situation worse, not better. He searched for an innocuous topic. "Do you...do you visit Phoenix often?"

Mari almost seemed to sigh in relief as she snatched at his conversational gambit. "Not often.

Maybe once every month or two, when Kirby or I need something we can't find in Sedona. Mostly when Kirby needs something unusual for his experiments."

She paused, then asked, "Did you enjoy your trip to the big city?"

He pondered that for a moment. "I enjoyed it, yes."

"I think I heard a 'but' in there. Was there something you didn't like?"

"The dinner was marvelous. I don't remember ever having such a satisfying meal." Then again, his memory only went back a few days. "And I was pleasantly surprised at how simple it was to navigate the mysteries of the hotel room."

She smiled. "It's because you're smarter than the average stagecoach robber. You catch on quick." She slanted him a speculative glance. "I still sense some disappointment, though."

She was right, and he tried to identify the source of it. "I don't know why, but I thought things would be more advanced in 120 years. I expected to be more amazed, more astonished. Instead, most inventions are merely logical enhancements or developments of devices that existed in the 1800s."

"Like what?"

"For example, the telephone is a logical extension of the telegraph and cars are merely advanced carriages."

"I see your point, but there are many other advances we've made in the areas of space flight, medicine and communication that you haven't been exposed to yet. I didn't want to overwhelm you, but believe me we've made a lot of progress."

"Perhaps. It just appears that everyday living

seems to go on much as it did in my time. With a few more conveniences, perhaps, but basically it's the same."

She nodded. "You're probably right."

Mari seemed much more at ease now, and they fell into a companionable silence as the miles rolled by. Eventually she broke the silence by saying, "You never answered my question."

"What question was that?"

"Last night. When I asked if you would come along on my date with Jordan tonight."

Come watch Jordan enjoy her company, touch her, maybe even make love to her? His immediate reaction was a strong negative. He doubted Jordan would relish the idea of an audience, either. "Do you think that's wise?"

"I don't mean at the same table. Just in the same restaurant."

"Why?"

"Tonight will be very difficult. I'm already nervous about it."

"What is it you fear?"

"I *fear* Jordan dropping me like a hot potato." She shrugged, though the tone of her voice belied the casualness she tried to affect. "His parents don't like me."

"You think he'll jilt you because his parents want him to?" Charles asked unbelievingly.

"He might. They have quite a bit of influence over him."

"If they can sway him so easily, then...perhaps it's best that you part."

"No, it's not," Mari insisted. "Jordan needs to learn to stand up to them, to live his own life as he sees fit, not to meet some grand plan of theirs. But they can be very persuasive, and I need to ensure I can convince him otherwise.''

"You can do that without my help," Charles insisted.

"No, you have more confidence in me than I do. That's why I need you at the restaurant."

"I don't understand."

Mari sighed. "I'm not sure I do, either, but all I know is that when I'm around you I feel confident, whole, no longer a misfit. Your experiment worked."

"Wait—"

"I need you, Charles." She cast him a pleading glance. "I'll feel much better if you're nearby. Just knowing you're there and that you believe in me will give me the courage and self-assurance to fight for my life with Jordan."

When he was silent, she added, "Please?"

He sighed, unable to resist her pleading. "All right, I'll go, but I am concerned."

"About what?"

"I fear you may come to rely on me too much, become too dependent on me to provide you with the confidence you need. It should come from inside you, not from without. I won't be around much longer, you know. You'll have to learn to do without me."

"Yeah, I know. But while you *are* still around, I'm gonna use you to shore up my self-confidence any time it threatens to sag. That is, if you don't mind."

When he remained silent, she said in a more tentative voice, "*Do* you mind?"

"I don't mind helping you, but I fear my methods have been less than honorable."

"What do you mean?"

He hesitated, uncertain how to broach the subject. "I believe your newfound assurance comes from the realization that I find you...desirable."

Mari stared at the road for a few moments before responding. "All right, I admit it. That does have something to do with it. But regardless—"

"No. We cannot disregard the fact that you are an engaged woman and I am a married man. I have no right to desire you."

"Well, technically you're a widower, since your wife has been dead for about a hundred years." Her tone was light, teasing.

He let his voice remain stern. "Perhaps, but since you plan to return me to my own time, that logic does not apply."

Mari bit her lip. "I just don't want you to think what you've done is wrong."

"But it is. And no matter how much we might want to make it not so, it is still wrong." Softly he added, "How can you expect to reform me and make it endure, if we cannot even resolve this simple problem?"

She sighed. "You're right...again."

He chuckled. "Don't take it too much to heart. If I could stay, I would. Then, as a widower, I could pursue this attraction I feel for you. But it can never be."

"I know. Don't rub it in, will ya?"

They entered Sedona, and as if to punctuate her remark, Charles suddenly felt something strange in his abdomen, a thick, curling sensation that seemed to encompass all his vitals and tug.

With a sinking feeling, Charles realized what it was—the vortex was finally trying to reclaim him.

THE FIRST THING MARI did when she got home was check on Buster. She found him in the lab with Kirby, curled up on top of the computer monitor and batting at images as they crossed the screen. She shot Kirby a quizzical look as she picked up the kitten.

He went immediately on the defensive. "Trust me, Mari, I fed him and gave him water, just like you told me to. But he's been bugging me ever since you left. Putting him there is the only way I could keep him quiet."

Buster seemed very glad to see her, as he rubbed his head against her cheek and purred. "That's okay. I believe you—he's probably just lonely." She pierced Kirby with a look. "You didn't try any experiments on him, did you?"

"Of course not—I promised I wouldn't. Besides, I had the plant."

Charles chuckled behind her. "And how fared the begonia?" Though his tone was light, Mari heard a hint of urgency in it.

"I haven't had a chance to experiment on it yet. I've been refining my theory, trying to determine how long you have here."

Charles nodded, though he seemed oddly intent on Kirby's answer. Suddenly suspicious, Mari asked, "Has something happened, Charles?"

He hesitated, then said, "Yes. I've experienced a tugging sensation, as if the vortex is trying to pull me back."

She stopped stroking Buster to stare at Charles. "You didn't tell me that."

"It just happened not long ago—when we arrived in town."

Mari turned to Kirby, hoping he'd have an explanation, a solution. It was too soon—Charles couldn't leave yet.

Kirby nodded. "That must be what those surges are. I saw one in the fields not too long ago."

"A surge?" Mari repeated. "What does that mean?"

"The energies have been building up all morning. I wasn't sure what they were building up to, until all of a sudden it peaked about half an hour ago. That must have been when Charles felt it."

"And what about now?" she demanded. "What's it doing?"

"It seems to have expended all its force on that one unsuccessful pull. The energies have died back down now."

Charles interrupted. "Do you mean to say they are no more? That I will be left in peace?"

"No," Kirby said, "I'm afraid not. This isn't the first surge. It's just the first one you felt. And it won't be the last."

Relieved, Mari said, "Well, if they didn't make it this time—"

"No, that's not how it works. It's increasing. Each time it will become stronger, until it's eventually successful."

Afraid to ask but having to know, Mari queried, "How long will that be?"

Kirby shrugged. "I don't know yet. I'll have a better idea when the next peak comes."

He turned to look at Charles. "And it depends, too, on how successful this attempt was. How did it feel?"

Charles frowned. "As if a dull hook had been thrust into my vitals, with a slight tugging sensation."

Kirby nodded. "Not very effective, then. Well, we'll know more when the next surge happens."

"When will that be?" Mari demanded.

"I don't know—but this is more important than experimenting with the plant. I'll work on it."

Feeling a little miffed that Kirby was treating Charles more like a research subject than a human being, Mari said, "Let us know what you find out. In the meantime, I have some errands to run before dinner tonight."

"Oh, that reminds me," Kirby said. "Your boyfriend called and said he'd pick you up at seven."

"Did he say what restaurant he's taking me to?"

"No." Kirby had seemed pleased that he'd remembered the call, but now he turned anxious. "Was I supposed to ask?"

"No, that's all right. It's just that Charles needs to know where we're going—so he can come, too."

Kirby looked puzzled. "Charles is going on your date?"

"No, no. I just want him in the restaurant." Seeing Kirby's obvious confusion, Mari added, "Never mind why. I guess he'll just have to follow us."

Charles appeared amused. "How? On foot? A horse might be a little conspicuous and I haven't learned to drive, unless you trust me to learn in a few hours?"

"No, no," Mari said, horrified. "Besides, you don't have a license." She turned to Kirby with a speculative look.

"Oh, no," he said. "Don't look at me. I don't want to be a fifth wheel. Leave me out of your date."

"You won't be on my date," she repeated. "All you have to do is drive Charles to the restaurant and have dinner. Just because it's the same restaurant Jordan and I will be eating in doesn't mean you're on our date.''

''You know I hate eating in those fancy places,'' Kirby whined.

''Oh, come on. It's just for one night. It won't kill you to dress up a little and have a nice meal.'' When he still looked stubborn, Mari said, ''Please? For me? I really need Charles there. And you can talk to him about his experiences with this time hook.''

Kirby sighed. ''Oh, all right. But don't expect us to sit with you and Jordan.''

She grinned and hugged Kirby. ''Don't worry, I won't. I don't even want him to know you're there.''

Mari spent the rest of the afternoon running errands, which kept her mind off the upcoming evening. But that changed as the time neared and she dressed for the date.

This was too important to her future to screw it up. The evening was bound to be difficult after that disaster of a dinner party, but she couldn't wimp out. She had to stand up for her parents while encouraging Jordan to stand up to his. If she didn't do that now, she'd set a bad precedent that would last throughout their marriage.

The tricky part was going to be accomplishing it without jeopardizing their engagement. And while she was at it, she might as well press Jordan for a wedding date. She'd feel far more confident about their impending nuptials if he would show some kind of commitment.

She sighed. Well, at least Charles would be there. She wasn't sure why she was so adamant that he come. After all, she'd even felt a little uncomfortable around him this morning after their heavy petting session the night before. But no matter how jumbled her emotions, Charles always seemed to find a way to give her added confidence, to bolster her self-worth.

Maybe he was right. Maybe it was because she knew he found her desirable. She smiled to herself. The feeling was heady stuff—it would give anyone the power of self-assurance. She was certainly no exception. In fact, it gave her a little thrill every time she thought about Charles's obvious attraction to her.

But it didn't matter why. The fact is, he made her feel good—kind of like a good luck charm.

She finished getting ready and joined Charles and Kirby in the living room. Charles rose to his feet when she came in the room. "You look absolutely beautiful."

A quiet glow of satisfaction filled her. She'd found a simple white dress in her closet that she'd almost forgotten about, one that seemed a lot more attractive on her now that she'd changed her hair and makeup. Apparently Charles thought so, too.

"Thank you," she murmured. "And thank you both for doing this for me. I really appreciate it."

Kirby seemed a little uncomfortable, but Charles inclined his head graciously. "It is our pleasure."

The doorbell rang and before they could say any more, Mari reminded them, "Stay behind us all the way, but wait a while before coming in to make sure we're seated first, okay?"

"Trust me," Kirby said, "we got it."

"Good." Taking a deep breath, Mari went to answer the door.

"Good evening," Jordan said. "Are you ready to go?"

"Uh, sure," Mari said, though she thought wistfully of the compliments, flowers and luxurious transportation Charles had lavished on her the previous night. Sighing, she realized that once again the practice date was unlikely to resemble the real thing.

She dawdled on the way to Jordan's car and fidgeted with her seat belt to give Kirby plenty of time to follow. When Jordan pulled away from the curb, she glanced in the rearview mirror, relieved when she saw Kirby's car following them.

To keep Jordan from noticing, Mari tried to distract him with the first thing that popped into her mind. "Uh, how was your day?"

"Not bad. And yours?"

"Okay. Lots of errands. Boring."

"What about yesterday?"

"Yesterday?"

"Yes, I called and Kirby said you were down in Phoenix...with that cousin of yours."

Did she detect a little annoyance in his voice? "Yes, uh, for research. Kirby needed us to look some things up for him at the library."

"Did it require both of you?"

"No, not really. But Charles had never seen Phoenix, so—"

"And you spent the night there?"

"Yes, but in separate rooms." She turned to stare at him in sudden realization. "Why, Jordan, you sound jealous." Maybe there was hope for him after all.

"Jealous? Don't be silly." His tone was flat, uncompromisingly so.

Well, he certainly squashed that idea. How galling to think that he wouldn't even be jealous of her, his own fiancée. "If you're not jealous, then what's the problem?"

Uh-oh, here came that condescending expression of his. "Now, dear, you know how we have to watch our reputation."

"We?" Her eyes narrowed. "You mean me, don't you?"

"Well, yes. Even in this day and age, a woman's reputation is more easily sullied than a man's. And spending the night in town with a man who isn't your fiancé can lead to all sorts of talk."

"In your social circle, maybe, but no one in mine would think a thing about it."

Jordan smirked at her. "Well, that's the point, isn't it? When we're married, you'll be in my social circle."

And what would happen to *her* friends? Granted, she didn't have many, but would Jordan snub them once they were married? Mari started to tell him he could fold his social circle into sharp angles and shove it up his outdated sense of propriety, but then she thought better of it. After all, the reason she was marrying him was to join that social circle...wasn't it?

Doubts assailed her, but they didn't linger long as they arrived at the restaurant and Jordan showed her inside. The maître d' paid a flattering amount of attention to them and showed them to a table right away. She seated herself in the chair he held for her before she thought.

Damn. Now Jordan was facing the door and could see Charles and Kirby arrive. "Wait," she said, causing Jordan to pause halfway into his chair. "Would you trade seats with me, please?"

"Trade?"

"Yes. I, uh, don't want to sit with my back to the door." *Oh, yeah. Smooth move, Marigold. Now you sound like a seedy private detective in a bad movie.*

Jordan gave her an odd look but complied—just in time to miss Charles and Kirby's arrival. Relieved that encounter had been averted, she tried to divide her attention between them and Jordan. Jordan asked her a question and she had no choice but to ignore him as she realized the waiter was leading Charles toward the table next to theirs. Horrified, she shook her head frantically.

"Well, what *would* you like, then?" Jordan asked, sounding perturbed.

When Charles sidetracked the waiter and apparently charmed him into seating them at another table behind Jordan, Mari relaxed and turned back to Jordan. "I'm sorry, what?"

"If you don't like the wine I've suggested, then what would you like?"

"I'm sure what you suggested would be fine."

Jordan looked confused. "But you just shook your head."

Good Lord, what else had he asked her? "No, I was just...shaking my head to...get rid of the, uh, ringing in my ears."

She felt like sinking with embarrassment. What an idiotic thing to say. No one could accuse her of thinking fast on her feet.

Jordan didn't seem to notice. "Ringing? Maybe you'd better not have wine, then. You don't want to upset your equilibrium if you're having ear problems."

"You're probably right," she answered, trying not

to peer past him to see what Charles and Kirby were doing. Besides, it seemed she'd need a clear head to survive this evening without mishap.

As they exchanged small talk, Mari couldn't help but smile to herself. Charles's imitation of Jordan had been right on the button the night before. Jordan did tend to affect an air of disdain and speak through his nose. Why hadn't she noticed that before?

She stole a glance at Charles, wishing she could share her amusement with him. He gave her a hearty thumbs-up. She smiled, wondering where he'd picked up that gesture. Probably from Kirby.

"Is something amusing?" Jordan asked.

"No," Mari prevaricated, "I'm just having a good time."

Despite herself, her gaze wandered back to Charles. He seemed engrossed in a conversation with a very attractive waitress who seemed to be putting the make on him. And Kirby, damn it, was doing nothing to stop it. In fact, he was watching with interest, almost as if he were observing the mating habits of another species. For heaven's sake, she wouldn't put it past him to take out pen and paper and begin taking notes.

"What's so interesting behind me?" Jordan asked.

Before he could turn around to look, Mari grabbed his sleeve. "Oh, nothing. Jordan, we have to talk."

He returned his attention to her. "I thought we were talking."

She released his sleeve, glad her gambit had worked. And since it had, she might as well make the most of it. "Yes, but I mean we should talk about what happened the other night...at the dinner party."

"Oh. That."

"Yes, that. I think we need to discuss it."

He dabbed at his mouth with his napkin. "Well, I spoke to my parents about it."

"You did?" Hope rose within her. Had Jordan taken her side?

"Yes, and Mother is quite miffed."

"About what?"

"I told her the truth about your mother's philanthropic endeavors and your father's high standing in the artistic community."

Mari was beginning to feel quite miffed herself. "And that made her upset? The fact that my parents are respectable?"

"No, no, you misunderstand. It's because *you* didn't tell her about it."

"I tried to, but she wouldn't listen." Myra Sloan had been too busy making snap judgments to listen to anyone. Glancing at Charles to bolster her courage, Mari said, "Besides, I'd just met her myself. Why didn't *you* tell her?"

"I didn't think it was my place."

"Well, after I tried to stand up for my parents and yours persisted in treating them like uneducated slobs, I gave up." If they couldn't be polite, they deserved what they got.

Jordan's lips flattened into a thin line. "I can see we're not going to agree about this. Perhaps we should change the subject."

She glanced at Charles again for inspiration but the damned waitress was hanging all over him, making him laugh and giving him the most obvious come-on Mari had ever seen. Annoyed, she snapped at Jordan, "And maybe we shouldn't."

When Jordan's eyebrows rose, Mari moderated her tone. Covering his hand with hers, she said earnestly,

"We should do what's right for us—not what's right for your parents...or mine. Don't you agree?"

He looked skeptical, so she continued. "You've been trying to escape their influence for ages, to become your own person. To become part of a couple. That's what we dreamed of for so long, isn't it?"

He frowned, but said, "Yes, I know I said—"

"And in order to do that, you need to stand up to them, for what you believe in."

With sudden insight, Mari realized much of Jordan's attraction to her had been her wide-eyed adoration. The more she admired him, the more he liked her. And when her interest waned, so did his. She gave him a tender smile and laid her hand on his. "Won't you stand up for me, Jordan?"

Jordan's indecisive expression faded and he gave her a genuine smile. "You're right. That's what I need to do. I won't let them come between us."

In triumph, Mari couldn't resist glancing over Jordan's shoulder. The waitress had disappeared, presumably gone back to work, and Charles was watching her with a questioning look on his face. Discreetly she gave him a thumbs-up of her own. Mission accomplished.

Jordan glanced at her curiously and before she could stop him, looked over his shoulder to see Charles grinning at her.

His face set and hard, Jordan turned back to Mari. "What's *he* doing here?"

"He?"

"You know damn well who I mean. What's Charles doing here?"

"I, uh, guess he and Kirby wanted something to eat."

"And they just happened to show up at the same restaurant we did?"

Mari shrugged. "It's a small town."

Jordan threw down his napkin. "I've had about enough of that man. You were right. I need to stand up for what I believe in. Either you send him packing immediately or..."

Shocked at this new side of Jordan, Mari said, "Or what?"

"Or...or our engagement's off."

Chapter Ten

Mari stared at Jordan, her mouth agape. She knew she should close it, but he'd truly surprised her this time. "You're asking me to choose between you and my family?"

"Not your whole family, just—"

"Good evening," Charles said, interrupting. He gave Mari a concerned glance, and she realized he must have seen her distress and come over to help. "May we join you for dessert?"

Before Jordan could say no, Charles had appropriated one of the empty chairs and pulled Kirby into the other one. If she weren't so upset, Mari could almost laugh. Jordan appeared indignant and Kirby looked confused. Charles was the only one who seemed at ease. It figured.

Jordan began, "I'm afraid—"

"Is there some problem?" their waiter asked. He was accompanied by the flirting waitress, who appeared as bewildered as Kirby.

"There's no problem," Charles assured them and began to explain the situation.

In the ensuing confusion, Mari was able to calm down a little. Her first inclination had been to tell

Jordan exactly where he could put his ultimatum, but was that really what she wanted to do? It would spell the death of all her hopes and dreams. No, it wasn't worth it, no matter how good it would make her feel.

Finally Charles succeeded in sorting things out and pacified the restaurant personnel while having their desserts delivered to the table. When they left, Charles turned to her and asked gently, "Is something wrong?"

Jordan's face turned stony, but Mari couldn't see any reason why she shouldn't explain. "Jordan just ordered me to kick you out of the house or our engagement's off."

Charles's eyebrows rose and even Kirby stopped eating for a moment to stare at Jordan. Jordan reddened, but lifted his chin even higher.

"Don't worry," Charles said. "I'm going to be gone in a week or so, when this experiment is done. Right, Kirby?"

"Uh, that sounds about right," Kirby agreed, obviously reluctant to be dragged in on this conversation.

Jordan's expression turned even colder. "I'm afraid that's too late. By then, there will be irreparable damage to my fiancée's reputation."

"But as her cousin—"

"Not by blood," Jordan interrupted. "Besides, no one will believe that."

Unfortunately they'd be right. Charles's speculative glance seemed to say the same thing. "I wouldn't do anything to harm Mari's reputation, but—"

"He can stay with me," Kirby said, spooning a bite of his dessert.

Three sets of eyes swung to stare at him, and Kirby

seemed to squirm under their combined attention. He shrugged. "Charles can stay at my house," he reiterated.

Knowing how much he hated having houseguests, Mari was touched. "Thank you, Kirby. That will solve everything."

Kirby nodded, then stabbed his spoon toward her. "But that doesn't include Buster."

"Buster?" Jordan asked. "Who's he?"

"Just a kitten," Mari explained.

"Well, Charles should take his cat with him," Jordan said.

"It's not Charles's cat," she explained, "it's mine."

"Yours? Since when did you get a cat?"

"Since a few days ago. He just sort of showed up on my doorstep." No sense explaining about time experiments and stuff.

"Well, get rid of it," Jordan insisted.

"Why? Does it bother you to know *he's* been sleeping with me?"

His mouth twisted in a grimace. "It sleeps with you?"

Apparently her sarcasm was wasted. "Yes. He's just a kitten, for heaven's sake."

"And I'm allergic to cats," Jordan explained with more force than she'd ever seen him use before.

At a loss, Mari merely said, "Oh." In the short time she'd had the little furball, she'd become attached to him. How could she get rid of him and leave him to run the streets at risk of being used for time experiments...or worse?

Smugly Jordan asked, "So you'll get rid of it?"

"I'll think of something," Mari soothed. Even if

she had to bathe the cat every day or give Jordan allergy shots, she was keeping Buster. But now was not the time to put her foot down. She'd save that battle for later.

"So," Charles said, beaming, "everything's resolved."

Jordan didn't look appeased. "No, it's not."

"Why not?" Mari demanded.

"Charles will still be in the same house with you, if he stays with Kirby."

"No," Mari explained patiently, "he'll be next door."

"But with that duplex, it's like living in the same house."

"No, it's like living next door," she repeated, feeling as though she'd regressed to kindergarten.

"I'm sorry," Jordan said with finality, "but that's still unacceptable."

Where did he get off changing the rules? "But Kirby has been living next door for years. You never objected to him. Do you want Kirby to move, too? Out of his own house?"

"No, no," Jordan assured her. "That's different."

Kirby regarded him quizzically. "How is it different? I'm not even related to her, so it seems it would be worse, not better."

It was Jordan's turn to squirm under three pairs of questioning eyes. Mari knew what he was thinking—that no one would think Kirby was a threat, but Charles was an entirely different matter. With wicked satisfaction, she also realized he couldn't say that without offending Kirby. And he had no reason to do that.

"I see your point," Jordan admitted. "But what will people think?"

With a devilish gleam in his eye, Charles reentered the conversation. "Am I correct in assuming it's only other people's opinions you are concerned about? You do trust your own fiancée, don't you?"

"Why, yes, of course," Jordan said in an insincere tone. Then again, how else could he answer?

"And you're a Sloan—a leader in your social set, correct?"

"I wouldn't put it quite that way," Jordan said, but his flattered smile belied his words.

"Ah, but your word and acceptance should carry a great deal of weight, especially as her fiancé. Am I correct?"

Mari didn't know where Charles was leading, and apparently neither did Jordan. Warily he answered, "Yes, I suppose."

Charles grinned. "Then if you invite Mari's next-door neighbors—Kirby and me—to your birthday party and show the world *your* acceptance of the situation, everyone should follow your lead. Isn't that right?"

"Well, I'm not sure."

Charles slapped him on the back. "Oh, but I am. That's it. We'll come, then, and you can put your seal of approval on the situation, then announce your engagement. You were planning to announce your engagement at the party, weren't you?"

Mari had to admire Charles's technique, as he had Jordan squirming in his chair. Even Kirby seemed amused.

Beads of perspiration broke out on Jordan's forehead. "I, uh, I mean *we* haven't discussed that yet."

"But there couldn't be a better time," Charles said heartily. "Don't you agree, Mari?"

Emphatically. It was about time Jordan made a public commitment. "That's a wonderful idea," she exclaimed. "Then you can show your parents you're really serious about marrying me."

Jordan looked as though he'd been backed into a corner. "Uh, yeah. Right. We'll announce it then." His words were as unenthusiastic as his expression. That was all right. Mari still had time to work on him before the party and convince him this was his idea.

"Good," Charles exclaimed. "So when's the wedding?"

Mari had to choke back her chuckle as Jordan looked even more hounded. He sputtered, "We haven't set a date yet."

Charles feigned shock, though there was a gleam in his eye. "You haven't? Well, maybe you should before someone else snatches her away from you, like…Benjamin."

Before Jordan could respond, Charles said, "Are you ready to leave, Kirby? Perhaps we should leave these two alone to work out the details of their coming nuptials."

Kirby and Charles departed, leaving confusion in their wake.

Jordan turned to her and asked, "Who's Benjamin?"

"Oh, no one."

"No one? Your cousin doesn't seem to think so."

"Really, he doesn't exist. Charles just made him up. I don't know anyone named Benjamin."

"Why would he do that?"

"I don't know—Charles is quite a rogue. Maybe he wanted to make you jealous."

Jordan gazed at her for a moment, then said slowly, "Maybe we *should* set a wedding date."

Mari could barely repress a grin. Charles's ruse had worked.

THE NEXT DAY, CHARLES decided to execute his move to Kirby's without delay. He had done enough to jeopardize Mari's engagement already. He didn't want to do anything to make it worse and ruin any chance she had for happiness.

As he gathered his few belongings together, Mari came to assist him. Giving him a remorseful look, she said, "I'm so sorry. This is silly."

Charles shrugged. "It doesn't matter. I don't want to do anything to sow dissension in your relationship with Jordan."

"If only he weren't so difficult," she said as she gathered an armful of clothes.

"Perhaps it's for the best," Charles said.

As they carried his few belongings to Kirby's house, Charles reflected that if they were honest they would have to admit Jordan had a point. They were more than a little attracted to each other, and their propinquity only reinforced that. Perhaps a little distance would allow them to resist this attraction.

The room at Kirby's was much like the one at Mari's, though it had a great many boxes stacked around the room. Equipment, no doubt, for Kirby's experiments.

Mari fussed around the room, trying to make Charles comfortable. "I'll ask Kirby to move those boxes right away."

"Don't bother. They aren't in my way—I spend so little time there, and I shall be gone soon, anyway." The depressing thought cast a pall on the room.

They finished arranging his clothes and Mari said, "I forgot to thank you for last night."

"It was the least Kirby and I could do to support you."

"No, I don't mean coming to the restaurant, though I do appreciate it. I wanted to thank you for rescuing me. When Jordan gave me his ultimatum, I didn't know what to do."

Relieved, he asked, "You aren't upset with me for interfering?"

"No, of course not. You kept a bad situation from getting worse. But...whatever possessed you to needle Jordan into setting a wedding date?"

"I thought he might need a little prodding."

"True. He did." Mari grinned. "But...Benjamin? Who is Benjamin?"

Charles returned her smile. "Just a figment of my imagination—it was the first name that occurred to me. Did it work?"

"Yes, strangely enough it did. Jordan didn't believe me when I assured him Benjamin didn't exist and suddenly he became eager to set the date."

Charles steeled himself against the pain. Mari seemed happy, so it was all worth it. "When is it? Shall I be here to witness your marriage?"

"No, it won't be for another six months."

"Six months? Why so long?" Would all his maneuvering be for naught?

"It takes a lot of time to plan a large wedding," Mari said defensively.

Yes, plenty of time for Jordan to change his mind. "Is a large wedding important to you?"

Mari thought for a moment, then said, "No, not really. It's the end result that counts. But Jordan seems to think his family will expect it."

"It sounds like a great deal of stress and anxiety. Are you sure you want to go through that? Why don't you just elope?"

"I—I hadn't thought about it."

"Perhaps you should. Six months is a long time—time for the Sloans to work on their son and convince him not to wed you."

Mari frowned in thought. "You're right. And I don't think Jordan will object too much. He seemed a bit overwhelmed at the thought of a large wedding himself. Thanks, Charles, I'll talk the idea over with him."

She paused, then continued, "I'm curious. Why on earth did you invite yourself to Jordan's birthday party?"

"After the problems you had with Jordan's parents and with your fiancé's..." how could he say this without being rude "...less than enthusiastic support, I thought you might need a champion there."

"I probably will. But I'm not sure Kirby shares your sentiments."

Charles had to grin. "Truth to tell, he wasn't overcome with excitement when I volunteered him."

"I can imagine."

"But he thinks a great deal of you, Mari, and wants to see you happy—even if it means spending an evening drinking and dancing among strangers."

"How kind of him to sacrifice himself so," she drawled.

"He thinks so." They shared a glance of fond amusement. "Actually Kirby and I had a very nice chat over dinner. He is working on a great many interesting projects."

Mari shot him an irritated glance. "He *should* be working on your problem."

"He is—along with several others, too. I don't think Kirby could work on only one thing at a time. And to follow your own advice, we should be working on *your* problem so we can eliminate the Sloans' objection to you—me. Let's take a look at those books."

"Good idea."

Charles followed Mari back to retrieve a couple of the books, then turned to leave.

"Where are you going?" she asked.

"Back to Kirby's."

"Don't be silly. We'll continue to work here, like we have been doing."

"But Jordan—"

"He's concerned about where you sleep, not where you work. Come on, let's get to work. We'll use the dining room this time—the table there is bigger than the one in the kitchen."

He shrugged. It was Mari's decision. Soon they had spread their books and notes across the entire dining-room table, and Charles opened one of the books about Black Bart. He had just barely begun to read when the doorbell rang.

Mari went to answer it, and Charles continued to read. Soon he heard footsteps approaching. He could only see a portion of the hallway from his vantage point, but he looked up in curiosity. Jordan's face appeared in the doorway, his expression changing to one of perverse triumph.

Entering the room, he gestured at Charles and said, "I thought you said he was going to move."

Mari followed him into the room. "He did—we moved his things to Kirby's this morning." Her eyes narrowed and she pierced Jordan with a suspicious glare. "Is that why you came by? To check up on me?"

"No, no, of course not," Jordan exclaimed in a tone Charles didn't find believable.

Apparently more than a little miffed, Mari grabbed Jordan's arm and dragged him off to the bedroom Charles had recently vacated. Charles followed and watched with a grin as Mari said, "See? His things are gone."

Jordan tried to act as if he didn't care, but his gaze darted all around the room, looking for evidence. "I...see," he said reluctantly.

Mari must have seen it, too, for she said, "You don't believe me. What's the matter, Jordan? You want to check out my room, too? You think maybe Charles moved in with me?"

Mari's anger must have finally registered with Jordan, for he quickly changed his attitude. "No, no, that won't be necessary." His voice took on a pleading tone. "I'm sorry, dear, but think how it looks. If he's moved out, why is he still here?"

"We're working." She dragged him back to the dining room and made a broad gesture to encompass the table.

With the books and notepapers spread across its surface, it should be evident to anyone what they were doing—even the slow-witted Jordan. Charles watched in amusement, waiting to see what he would do next.

When Jordan remained silent, Mari said, "This is my job. You don't mind if I do that, do you? I have to earn a living."

"Once we're married, you won't need to work—I'll support you."

My, my, that was the wrong thing to say. Mari might be shy, but she was also very independent. Didn't Jordan realize that?

"Support me?" Mari repeated incredulously. "On what? You don't work."

"No, not yet. But I'm taking a position in my father's bank right after my birthday. Besides, I have a very generous allowance—there's no need to worry."

Mari seemed to deflate suddenly. "Oh, Jordan. Are you sure they'll continue your allowance once you're married?"

She didn't say it, but Charles heard the rest of her unspoken sentence in his head—especially since Jordan was marrying Mari.

Jordan looked shocked. "You think they might disinherit me?"

"Maybe—if you marry me."

What was Mari doing? Was she *trying* to sabotage her relationship? Before Jordan could react, Charles decided to intervene. In a cheerful tone, he said, "Then don't marry him. You can always marry Benjamin."

Mari shot him a glance that was half amused, half exasperated, but Charles was unperturbed. He knew what he was doing.

Jordan's expression turned suspicious. "You told me Benjamin wasn't real."

Mari sighed. "He's not. Charles is just pulling your leg."

At Jordan's skeptical look, Charles said, "Benjamin's not real? Oh, I forgot. Quite right. He doesn't exist."

Mari's fiancé didn't look at all convinced. Turning to Mari, he said, "Well, Benjamin or no Benjamin, you won't need to marry anyone else." He shot a triumphant glance at Charles. "You're marrying me."

Charles smiled back, though he hated the thought of the two of them wed. For Mari, he reminded himself. He was doing this for Mari. "Good. I'm glad that's settled. So, when are you buying her a ring?"

Jordan looked stunned. "A ring?"

"Yes. Isn't it customary to provide your betrothed with a ring as evidence of your devotion?"

Mari seemed hard put to stifle a smile. Jordan, however, didn't seem to suspect that Charles was manipulating him.

"Oh, yes, a ring." The puzzled look on Jordan's face cleared. "My grandmother left me her wedding set for my future wife. It has a beautiful diamond."

Mari's face lit up. "Oh, Jordan, your grandmother's ring? That sounds perfect."

"Good," Charles exclaimed. "When are you going to present it to her?"

Jordan thought for a moment. "I need to get it out of the safety deposit box and have it cleaned. I know—I'll give it to you on my birthday, when we announce our engagement. How does that sound?"

Jordan seemed pleased, almost as if he'd thought the idea up himself.

Mari beamed at him. "That sounds perfect. Now, why did you come by?"

"Huh?"

"If you weren't checking up on me, why did you come by?"

"Well, I, uh, I just wanted to...to tell you about...the ring. That's it." He smiled in relief and satisfaction. "I wanted to tell you about the ring— and remind you my birthday party is only a few days away."

"Good," Mari said. She patted his arm, then led him toward the door. "And now that you've told me, maybe we can get back to work."

Jordan frowned and tossed a suspicious glance over his shoulder, but Charles merely smiled at him.

Mari led him inexorably toward the door. "The sooner we finish this job, the sooner Charles can leave."

That seemed to dissolve the remainder of Jordan's objections, and he exited.

When Mari entered the dining room, Charles grinned at her. "That was smoothly done."

She chuckled. "I learned it from you. And thanks to you, I'm also finding it easier to feel comfortable around Jordan—less klutzy."

Pleased that he could assist her in such a small way, Charles murmured, "I'm glad."

"So am I—you've managed to not only convince Jordan to set a wedding date but to give me an engagement ring."

At least she was going to be happy. Charles kissed her on the brow. "You deserve the best of everything."

Instead of shying away, Mari gave him a quick hug, saying, "Thank you."

He released her with reluctance, not willing to jeopardize all he had just accomplished. They went back to work and soon Charles was immersed in the story of Black Bart and the intrepid lawman who had tracked him.

The story was hauntingly familiar, and when Charles came across a picture of Black Bart after he was caught he was shocked. The man looked so old. He studied the photograph carefully. It looked familiar, but the man's bushy mustache and hat disguised his face, making it difficult for Charles to ascertain which features they shared in common. Some other things didn't add up, either.

"Mari, come over here, would you?"

As she looked over his shoulder, he pointed to the page. "That's a picture of Black Bart after he was captured. Does it look like me?"

Mari studied it "It's hard to tell. The man in this picture is much older, but it could be you."

"That's the problem. I'm not much older in this picture. According to this book, I must have been thirty-nine when you picked me up in 1874, and forty-eight when I was captured. Could I have aged so much in only nine years?"

Mari looked as puzzled as he felt. "I suppose it's possible."

"But—do I look thirty-nine to you?"

"No, you look ten years younger."

"How do you explain the discrepancy, then?"

Mari shrugged. "I'm not sure. Maybe we got the date wrong and pulled you in even earlier than we expected."

"No, that doesn't accord with the facts. I remember too much about Black Bart after he became an outlaw."

"Well, maybe it was the time-travel process itself, then," Mari suggested. "Maybe traveling through time reversed some of the aging process."

Charles nodded slowly. That could account for the facts.

Mari grinned. "Maybe we just discovered a cure for old age." She paused, then said, "Hey, wait a minute. Did you just say you *remembered*?"

"Yes, but I'm afraid it will do you no good."

"Why not?"

"You remember that poem I recited the other day?"

"Yes."

"It was written *after* I began robbing stages." He gestured down at the book. "And I remember reading these newspaper stories, too."

"But...that's not possible."

"I'm afraid it is," he said gently, "if you assume I read them *after* they were printed."

Mari turned her shocked face to his. "But that means—"

"Yes, I'm afraid so. It's too late to reform me. I've already begun to steal."

Chapter Eleven

Mari stared at Charles in stunned silence. After all they'd been through, it was too late? "You're already Black Bart? How can that be?"

"I don't know, but the evidence is plain. I knew what those newspaper articles were going to say before I read them. I must have read them before."

"So if we picked you up later than 1874, when was it?"

Charles shrugged. "I don't know. I still don't have my memory back."

"Maybe Kirby can shed some light on this."

They brought their books along and found Kirby in his accustomed place in the lab. He looked up when they walked in and said, "Good. There you are. I was just working on your problem."

Mari frowned. "We have a different problem now, Kirby."

"What's that?"

"Charles remembers too much of his life *after* 1874."

Kirby frowned. "That would mean he came from later in time."

"We figured that out," Mari said, exasperated.

"But trust me, that's impossible. At least, I think it is." Kirby's brow creased in a worried frown as he typed furiously on the keyboard. Finally his brow cleared, and he said, "Everything checks out here. Are you sure about this?"

Charles nodded. "I remember newspaper articles that couldn't have been written until after the first robbery."

"There's something else strange, too," Mari interjected. "If we picked him up in 1874, he should be thirty-nine years old. But with what he remembers, he has to be older than that. Look at him. Does he look forty to you?"

Kirby peered at Charles. "I'm not very good at guessing ages—"

"Then take my word for it—he doesn't. He looks much younger. How do you explain that?"

"I don't know. My research only covered the actual time-travel process itself, not the effects of the process on the subject. But I have figured out how to send him back with his clothes."

Mari waved that away as irrelevant. "Well, I have a theory I'd like to run by you. Is it possible that yanking him through time took ten years off his age?"

"It doesn't seem likely."

"But it is probable?"

"I couldn't say without further research. A year ago, I wouldn't have believed time travel was possible. At this stage, anything's probable."

"Okay, so is it also possible that by bringing him through time, you pulled him through the rest of his life so he experienced all of it on the way? And that it was so overwhelming it caused him to black out and lose his memory? It would explain why he remembers things after 1874.''

Kirby blinked at her. "Have you been reading science fiction again?''

"No, I—''

"It's an interesting theory, but too complicated. Have you ever heard of Occam's Razor?''

"No.''

"Occam's Razor postulates that the simplest explanation is the most likely.''

"And the simplest explanation is…?''

Reluctantly Kirby said, "If Charles remembers events after 1874, then I miscalculated somehow.'' He stared at the computer screen, then shook his head, muttering, "But I don't know how I could have. I've checked all my figures and they seem just fine.''

Suddenly impatient, Mari said, "Okay, I didn't really believe my theory anyway. So, can you send him back in time before he performs his first robbery, so he can talk himself out of it?''

Kirby stared at her, shocked. "Two of him, occupying the same time? I don't know what would happen, but it could be dangerous. *Very* dangerous. The paradoxes associated with such an occurrence could tear apart the whole time continuum—or Charles himself.''

Mari frowned. "Well, forget that idea, then.''

Kirby turned to Charles. "Do you have any idea what year we picked you up from?''

"No.''

"What does it matter?'' Mari asked. "If he's already Black Bart, it's too late.''

Kirby stared at her earnestly. "Not necessarily. If

he hasn't been arrested yet, the world won't know who Black Bart really is.''

Sudden hope lit within her. ''Yes! Charles, did the articles that speak of your arrest seem familiar?''

''I'm not sure. Some accounts are very clear—the poems for instance. Others are fuzzy, as if I'm not quite sure I've read them. I'm sorry, I don't know.''

Kirby frowned. ''How about the location, then? Do you know how often you visited Funk Hill? That's where we snatched you from.''

Charles shook his head. ''I don't remember that much—''

''Wait,'' Mari exclaimed. ''I remember reading that you only pulled two robberies on Funk Hill. One of them was your first holdup...and the other was your last. So if we didn't pick you up at the first...''

Charles finished for her. ''You must have picked me up at the last robbery. But was that before or after I did the deed?''

Excited, Mari said, ''I'd say before.''

''Wishful thinking?'' he asked.

''No—the books say you were winged in that last robbery by a bullet. Since you didn't show up here with any damage, it must have been before the robbery.''

Charles nodded slowly, but Kirby said, ''You're ignoring another possibility—that he might not be Black Bart at all. We might have picked up one of the other people on the coach, like the driver or a passenger.''

Charles shook his head. ''Your Occam's Razor applies here as well. A random driver or passenger would be unlikely to have as much knowledge and memory of Black Bart as the real Charles Boles.''

Kirby nodded reluctantly. "True, plus I just remembered that the machine registered only one life-form."

Mari flipped through the book she still held in her hand. "The reason Black Bart was caught is because he dropped his handkerchief at the last robbery after he was shot. The laundry mark led the detectives to him. If we can just make sure you don't drop that handkerchief..." She paused, thinking. "The problem is, the trip through time will leave you disoriented and you'll probably lose your memory again. And even if we can keep you from robbing the stage that time, how will we prevent you from doing it later?"

"That's easy," Kirby said. "We'll send a note back with him."

"But if his clothes don't go back, will the note?"

"Yes, it will. Remember, I told you earlier I solved the clothes problem."

"Oh, that's right." She brightened. "You know, that might work. If he goes back with a note in hand, he'll probably read it before he does anything else. We can warn him."

"How will that help?" Charles asked. "I won't be reformed—I'll still be Black Bart."

"Yes, but if you don't get caught, no one will connect Charles Boles with Black Bart."

Charles nodded. "That is, if you can convince the 'me' I was then not to rob again."

Mari grinned. "We'll give you a reason not to. Black Bart only took to robbing stages when gold mining didn't work. If we find a vein that wasn't discovered yet and give you directions to it, you won't have any need to steal."

Charles nodded. "That might do the trick."

Unfortunately it also meant he wouldn't have any need to remember her. Selfishly she wanted him to. "And we can continue to work on restoring your memory in this time, in the hope that it will make it easier to remember your time here when you get back to the past."

Charles smiled warmly at her. "Yes, I do want to recall my time here."

His gaze sent a wave of heat across Mari's face. She wanted that, too.

A sudden peculiar expression crossed Charles's face. "What's wrong?" she asked.

"It's the tugging sensation. I believe the vortex is surging again."

Kirby glanced at his monitor. "Yes, it registered here, too. How severe was it?"

"About half again as strong as the last."

Kirby nodded. "That tracks with my calculations."

Urgently Mari said, "How much time does he have left?"

Kirby punched a few keys, then said, "My estimates are a little more accurate now, with this additional data. I'd say four days, tops."

Four days? Stunned, Mari tried to take it in. No, it was too soon.

Charles gave her a sickly smile. "At least I shall be here to attend Jordan's birthday party with you."

The importance of the party paled in comparison to the thought of losing Charles. Well, she couldn't do anything about that, but she'd be damned if she'd let him go without trying to ensure he remembered her, too. "We don't have much time to lose, if we're going to help you regain your memory. We'll have to find a faster way of doing this."

"How about hypnosis?" Kirby asked.

"That might work, but we don't have time to search for a hypnotist, unless you know of someone."

"Yes," Kirby said. "Me."

"You?"

"I had a psychology course at college that demonstrated its uses. Fascinating."

She shouldn't have been surprised. One of the reasons Kirby was so successful was that he tapped the knowledge of the soft—or fringe—sciences, such as sociology and metaphysics, and combined them in unique ways with the hard sciences. "So you can hypnotize Charles?"

"I think so. I observed more than I participated, but the application seems simple."

Mari turned to Charles. "Are you willing to be hypnotized? I believe they called it mesmerism in your day."

"I'm aware of what it entails," Charles said, "though I'm unfamiliar with the risks associated with it."

Kirby frowned. "The biggest risk is that it may not work at all, or the power of suggestion may implant false memories in you, which can seem as true as the real thing. I'm not skilled at this, so I'm uncertain how successful the experiment will be."

Charles nodded thoughtfully. "I see. Either way, I will be no worse off than I am now, and since there is the chance that it will lead to the resumption of my memory I'm willing to try it."

"Good," Kirby said, and looked around the lab. "This isn't the best place for something like that. We need a place that's comfortable, with few distractions."

"How about my living room?" Mari asked.

"An excellent suggestion," Charles concurred. "There's little to distract me there, save for a few recent memories." He winked at her. "But I dare say I'll be able to overcome that limitation...if Mari co-operates."

Mari felt her face flame. Did he really think she would cuddle up to him while Kirby tried to hypnotize him? No, of course he didn't. He was just teasing her.

Kirby glanced back and forth between the two of them. Her blush and the twinkle in Charles's eyes were dead giveaways that something was going on between them. Trying to act nonchalant, Mari said, "Well, let's go to the living room, then."

Her serene exit was spoiled by tripping over one of the computer power cords. Charles caught her from falling on her face. He was there so fast, it was almost as if he knew she'd be klutzy. She darted him an annoyed glance and whispered, "You did this on purpose."

"What?" Charles answered in a low tone, though his voice was still teasing as he followed her into her house, his hand under her elbow. "I was only being truthful—I do have distracting memories of your living room, especially the sofa."

She did, too, unfortunately. "Well, try to forget them," she whispered back. "This is serious."

Charles just nodded, but the look in his eyes told her he hadn't forgotten and didn't intend to.

Behind them, Kirby said, "Why don't you sit on the couch and make yourself comfortable?"

Charles glanced at the couch, then at Mari. "Actually I think it would be better if I used the chair. It looks more…comfortable.''

"Fine, fine. Whatever,'' Kirby said, though his glance still darted curiously between Charles and Mari.

Maybe Kirby wasn't as oblivious to human interaction as she'd thought. It was just her luck that he would pick now to come out of his self-absorbed fog.

Kirby seated himself in the chair opposite Charles, leaving Mari with no place to sit except on the couch. Deliberately she chose the opposite end of the couch from where they'd snuggled, and tried to ignore Charles's knowing glance. Instead, she concentrated on Kirby.

"If you don't mind, I'd like to record this,'' Kirby said. "Charles should remember the session, but just in case, I'd like a record of it.''

Since Charles didn't object, Kirby switched on the recorder.

"Do you need some kind of pendulum or something to put him under?'' Mari asked.

"No, no. We just need to get him to relax.'' Over the next several minutes, Kirby spoke softly to Charles, encouraging him to unwind and to focus on nothing but the sound of Kirby's words.

Eventually Charles's shoulders slumped, his eyes drifted shut, and his face relaxed.

"Is he under?'' Mari whispered.

"Yes, but there's no need to whisper. I've told him to listen only to the sound of my voice until I bring him out of it.''

Mari nodded and motioned for Kirby to get on with it, feeling a bit of excitement. Why hadn't they thought of this before? It was their best chance to get Charles to regain his memory.

Kirby stared intently at Charles. "Charles, I want you to think back, back before we brought you to this time, back to the year 1874. Can you do that?"

Charles hesitated for a moment, then nodded.

"Good. Now, I want you to go back to a particular day. A day when you were happy there. Can you find such a day?"

"I'm not sure."

Kirby turned to Mari and whispered, "What did he do back then?"

"He was a gold prospector."

Kirby nodded. "Charles, I want you to concentrate on prospecting. Do you remember anything about mining for gold?"

Charles hesitated, then nodded.

"Tell us about it."

When he didn't say anything, Kirby whispered, "I guess I need to be more specific." Speaking to Charles, he asked, "Do you remember a typical day of gold mining?"

Charles nodded.

"Then tell us about it. Where are you?"

"In...California," he said in hesitation.

"And what is happening?"

In halting tones, Charles described the backbreaking work of the gold miner, the endless toil and sweat and the inevitable disappointment when no gold was found.

Mari listened in fascination to this slice of life from the past, but Kirby didn't seem impressed. When he frowned and shook his head, she asked, "What's wrong?"

"It doesn't sound like a real memory," Kirby whispered. "It sounds more like he's telling a story."

"Are you sure?"

"No, not really. Let's delve some more." In a louder voice, he said, "Charles, now I want you to come forward a few years, to the date of your first robbery."

"July 26, 1875," Mari whispered.

Kirby repeated the date for Charles's benefit. "You're waiting outside Copperopolis on Funk Hill and you hear a stagecoach approach. What happens next?"

In more confident tones, Charles related the colorful story. "As the driver approached, I pulled a brown flour sack over my head to disguise my features and entered the road, stopping the coach on an uphill grade so he would be unable to retreat easily. My sudden appearance frightened the lead horse, who halted. Shielding myself behind the horse, I pointed my shotgun at the driver, saying, 'Please throw down the box.'"

Mari grinned. Even while robbing a stage, he was polite.

"The driver hesitated," Charles continued, "so I said, 'If he dares to shoot, give him a solid volley, boys.'"

Kirby raised an eyebrow at Mari, then looked at Charles. "I thought you worked alone."

"I did, but I had fashioned sticks to appear as if they were rifles and my handiwork lay all around, leaving the driver to believe he was outnumbered."

"What happened then?"

"He had no choice but to throw down the express

box. But a lady passenger became distressed and threw her purse upon the ground.''

"What did you do?"

"I handed it back, telling her I was only interested in Wells Fargo's money. There is a code for highwaymen, you know."

"There is?"

"Yes, the possessions of women passengers are sacrosanct, as is the driver's personal wallet. It is the code of the road."

Kirby merely raised an eyebrow and continued. "Then what happened?"

"I ordered them to drive on, and another stage appeared. I ordered him to throw down his express box as well, but he swore it was a private stage, so I told him to drive on."

"And you believed him?"

"Yes," Charles reiterated. "Again, it was the code. Any man who did not abide by it, whether driver or robber, was summarily dealt with when his dishonor became known."

Mari couldn't help but feel a bit of pride that despite his thievery Charles had maintained his honor. He would be glad of that, too, when he remembered.

Kirby scowled once more, and Mari asked, "What's wrong?"

"It still sounds too pat."

"Even with all that detail?"

"Maybe. Is there anything he related that he could not have gotten from one of the books you read…or have extrapolated from what you knew of the time?"

"No," Mari answered reluctantly, "but that doesn't mean it isn't a true memory."

"It could be, but let me try a few more."

Slowly Kirby led Charles through accounts of additional robberies. They sounded authentic to Mari, but Kirby didn't seem satisfied. He took him to the last robbery and beyond—to his time in prison. Each was described with the same accuracy.

Mari watched in dismay. "We're too late," she said in despair.

"Not necessarily. Again, these are accounts he could have read about in your research."

In relief, Mari realized he probably had. "What now?" she asked.

"I'll try something he can't have read much about. What do you suggest?"

"I didn't see much mention of his wife and children beyond their names. Maybe you could ask about them."

Mari cursed herself. Why had she suggested that? Did she really want to know about the woman he had married, the woman who had borne his children?

Kirby turned back to Charles. "Charles, I want you to think about your wife." Turning to Mari, he whispered, "What was her name?"

"Mary."

He raised an eyebrow, but said only, "Charles, tell me about Mary."

Charles's mouth curved in a smile. "She is beautiful and shy, with lustrous brown hair that smells of springtime and soft brown eyes a man could drown in."

Mari listened helplessly as Charles catalogued the virtues of his wife, feeling jealous despite herself. If only someone would describe *her* that way. Someone? Hell, who was she kidding? If only Charles would describe her that way.

He continued to rhapsodize, concluding, "Though she is shy and womanly, she is fiercely protective. I remember a time when she saved a small kitten from her neighbor…"

Mari glanced at Kirby incredulously. "Is he…?"

"He's talking about you," Kirby confirmed.

Warmth spread through her as she tried to recall everything he'd said. Did he really think of her in that way? Surely he did—people couldn't lie under hypnosis, could they?

"This isn't working," Kirby said. "Let's bring him out of it."

Though reluctant to cut Charles off when he was just getting to the good stuff, Mari could see Kirby's point. Charles was getting Mari confused with his wife, so this wasn't working.

Slowly Kirby brought Charles out of his trance and asked, "Do you remember everything that happened?"

Charles considered for a moment, then said, "I believe so."

"Have you regained any of your memory?"

"No. All I recall well are the moments you queried me about. Why did you stop?"

"I don't think we were getting anywhere. They didn't seem like real memories, more like you parroting what you had learned from the books."

Charles nodded. "I suppose that's possible."

"And at the end, when I asked you to describe your wife, you talked about Mari instead."

Charles darted a quick glance at Mari who smiled back shyly. "You're correct, but that's what I thought you asked me to do."

Kirby glanced over at the tape recorder and

switched it off. Frowning, he said, "I may have at that." He replayed the last part of the tape. "You're right. The second time, I asked you to tell me about 'Mary,' but I didn't specify which one. Since they both sound alike, you chose the Mari you know here."

"So," Charles said, "the experiment is a failure."

"Not necessarily. It may be the fault of my questioning, not your memory. Let me replay the tape and see where I went wrong, then we can try again later."

Charles turned to Mari. "I'm sorry. I had hoped this would help. I do want to remember you."

"I do, too. I know I won't ever forget *you*." The look on Kirby's face was so odd Mari had to ask, "What's wrong, Kirby?"

"You haven't thought this through."

"What do you mean?"

"If this works and we send Charles back, then he'll change history."

"I know that. He won't be Black Bart anymore— and no one will ever know he was."

"And the ripple effect means that other things will change, as well. If no one ever knows he is Black Bart, then the Sloans won't know your father is related to him...because your father won't know. And if your father doesn't know..."

Realization dawned. "Then I won't know." She turned to pierce Kirby with a fierce glare. "Are you saying..."

"I'm saying that if this works in the new time line you won't have any need to bring Charles to the present. You'll never meet."

Chapter Twelve

She wouldn't remember? Sudden need flared within Charles. He wanted to grab her and kiss her senseless, to brand her with his essence so deep she would never be able to forget him.

He suppressed it. He had no right to do so—and it might startle Kirby, not to mention Mari.

Instead, he said, "Even if you won't remember me, at least I might recall you, providing I can retain my memory when I return to my own time." It hurt but would have to suffice.

"Oh, Charles," Mari said tearfully and came into his arms. "I don't want to forget you."

Kirby, appearing a little uncomfortable at Mari's display of emotion, backed out of the room, saying, "I, uh, I'm just going to review this tape..."

Wordlessly Charles led Mari to the sofa, where she sat next to him and laid her head on his shoulder. Sensing she wanted only comfort, he stroked her hair in a soothing motion.

"You've helped me so much," Mari said. "What will I do if I never meet you, never get to know you?"

"You were doing well before you met me. You

will again." And she certainly didn't need a rogue like him.

"But I wasn't. That's the reason we brought you here."

"If this works, you won't need me to feel confident and assured. The Sloans' acceptance will give you that."

"Will it?"

Charles couldn't answer that—only she could.

"Maybe," Mari said tentatively, "maybe we *shouldn't* reform you."

So she could remember him? Touched by her thought, Charles was nevertheless practical. "But you need me reformed in order to gain the support of your future in-laws. I'll be gone in a couple of days, never to return. You'll have them for the rest of your life."

"Is that a threat?"

He chuckled. "Think about it, Mari. Which is more important? Remembering a few days with a man you'll never see again or establishing the foundation for a happy life with your future husband?"

She gave him a lopsided grin. "Can I have a few moments to think about it?"

Ignoring her levity, he said, "We both know the answer. Your happiness is foremost."

"But why can't I have both?" Mari wailed.

"Because Time won't let you."

She sighed. "I know. You're right. But I don't have to like it."

"I don't care for it—" Charles broke off as Kirby entered the room, looking triumphant.

He waved the tape at them. "I have it. Boy, was I dumb. I asked you so many leading questions, it's a wonder we got any sense out of you at all."

Mari raised her head from Charles's shoulder. "What do you mean?"

"I made too many assumptions about who Charles is and what year he came from. I inadvertently set up expectations in him, so when he answered my questions he was answering to please me, not necessarily what he remembered." Kirby paused. "At least, that's how it sounds on the tape. Charles, do you remember what we discussed in the hypnosis session?"

"Yes."

"Were those real memories…or just vivid recreations of a possible history from your reading?"

"I don't know. I have so few real memories to compare them to."

"But it's possible they weren't true memories?"

"Yes, it's possible." It would account for the slight distance he felt when reviewing those "memories."

"Would you like to try it again?"

"Certainly." If it would help Mari, he was willing to do anything.

"Okay, but this time I'll let you hear Mari, in case she wants to ask questions."

Once again, Kirby put Charles under. Charles relaxed, letting Kirby lead him to a safe, secluded spot in his own mind. His tensions eased and he felt his eyes close as he drifted serenely.

"Charles?" Kirby asked.

"Mmm-hmm."

"What's your name?"

"Charles."

Kirby swore under his breath. "When did you first remember your name was Charles Boles?"

He searched his limited memory. "When Mari told me what it was."

"Do you remember hearing the name before that?"

"Yes."

Kirby paused, then asked, "In what capacity?"

"I read about him."

"Him?" There was another short pause, then Kirby asked, "Before we brought you to our time, were you Charles Boles?"

"No." The feeling was very strong. He didn't know how he knew, but he knew he wasn't Charles Boles.

Mari gasped and Kirby continued. "Were you Black Bart?"

The feeling was equally strong. "No."

"Can this be true?" Mari asked. "Or is it more wishful thinking?"

Charles answered. "It is not wishful thinking. I wish to be Black Bart."

"Why?" she demanded.

"So I can help you."

"Wait, Mari, let me continue," Kirby said. "Charles...or whatever your name is. What *is* your name?"

Charles hesitated. He knew the answer, yet it was hidden behind a veil he could not penetrate. He gave the only answer he knew. "My name is...Charles Boles."

"No," Kirby said patiently, "I mean, what was your name *before* we brought you to our time?"

Once again the answer was obscured behind a barrier he could not breach. "I can't remember."

"You know," Kirby mused, "none of this proves my calculations were incorrect. They have to be—the date has to be right. Charles...whoever...I want you to go back to the day before we brought you to the present. Go back to 1874. Are you there?''

Charles could picture the time in his mind. ''Yes.''

''Who are you?''

''No one.''

''No one? I mean, what's your name?''

''I don't know.''

''Are you Charles Boles?''

Again, the definite negative feeling. ''No.''

Kirby sighed. ''Maybe it's too close to the memory loss. Now go back ten years earlier, to 1864. Who are you?''

''No one.''

''Look around you. What do you see?''

''Nothing—just a formless gray void.''

''This isn't working. I'm going to bring you out of your trance.'' Slowly Kirby counted backward until Charles was fully awake.

He blinked at them, seeing the puzzlement on Kirby's face and the confusion on Mari's.

''You aren't Black Bart,'' she whispered.

''I know.'' He should be elated, but...

''Then...who are you?''

He shrugged, hating this helpless feeling. Before, he had at least an identity, albeit a nefarious one, to start with. But now he was once more adrift on an unknown sea of lost memories. Worse, he had no idea as to his origin or his true character.

''He could be anyone,'' Kirby said. ''Anyone passing Funk Hill at the time we snatched him. That explains the apparent age discrepancy anyway—without resorting to wild theories.'' Kirby appeared pleased that his Occam's Razor once again proved true.

Mari looked confused. "You mean...like a stage driver or a passenger?"

"No—I only picked up one life-form reading. He must have been alone."

Charles frowned. "Then...I may still be a thief."

"How can you say so?" Mari asked, sounding shocked.

"Why else would a lone man be on Funk Hill? According to the books, it was a notorious place for robbing stages."

"But it was a common thoroughfare," Mari said. "You could have been on horseback, just passing through."

"No," Kirby reminded her, "I only registered one life-form. No horse."

"Okay, then, he was *walking* through. That wasn't unheard of, was it? Black Bart did it all the time."

Charles nodded. "We have to concede either possibility."

"No," Mari insisted. "I won't believe you're a bad man, Charles. Nothing you've said or done here has indicated you have an evil bone in your body. Just the opposite. Why, even *you* couldn't believe you were a thief and a cad."

"Yes, but I can only hope I'm not. I *know* I'm not Black Bart."

"But, Charles..." Mari hesitated. "Your name may not even be Charles. What shall we call you?"

"Charles will do until we learn my real name. I've become accustomed to it."

"Then Charles it is," Kirby said with a bit of impatience. "Hey, let me go read up on hypnosis and memory. See if I can find anything that might help."

"All right," Charles said absently as Kirby exited.

Charles was more concerned with Mari's reaction. "How do you feel about this?"

"I'm...glad and sad."

"How so?"

"I'm glad you're not Black Bart, that you're not an outlaw." She turned a stubborn face to him. "And no matter what you say, I won't believe you're a bad person."

Charles had to smile. She was championing him as fiercely as she had young Buster.

"But I'm a little sad this was all for nothing," Mari said.

"Nothing? How can you say that?"

"Well, if you're not Black Bart, then I can't reform you. The Sloans will still hate me and I won't even remember you." She shook her head. "It was all for nothing."

"But you will remember me, now. Black Bart will still rob stages, will still be caught...unless I stop him."

Hope warred with indecision on Mari's face. "But—"

"You'll be sending me back to 1874, so I have a year to find him and convince him not to turn outlaw. We still have a chance to change history."

Mari punched him in the arm.

Shocked, he asked, "Why did you do that?"

"For jerking me around. First, you're Black Bart and I won't remember you, then I will remember you because you're not Black Bart, then I won't because you'll change history anyway. It's enough to make me crazy."

Her reasoning was convoluted, but Charles still followed it. He gathered her into his arms. "I'm sorry.

I don't mean to make you crazy. I just want what's best for you. And that's Jordan.'' Or so Mari thought.

She just sniffed.

"We've been over this before. This is best, isn't it?''

"I guess,'' Mari agreed, but she added to herself, *I still don't have to like it.*

"We only have a few days left to learn who I am." He squeezed her hand. "I had hoped we would have this solved by the party.''

"Well, it doesn't look like it's going to happen now. The odds are you're not going to regain your memory in the next couple of days.''

"I know. But it's going to be a great deal more difficult for you at the party if the Black Bart issue isn't resolved.''

How sweet. Here he was, without a memory, without a past, waiting to be yanked back through time, and his only thoughts were of her—how *she* was going to fare. Touched, she gave him a kiss on the cheek.

Kirby walked in at that moment and shot her a puzzled glance. "Uh, Mari, did you ever think that maybe Jordan isn't the right person for you?''

Mari grimaced. "Subtle, Kirby, real subtle.''

He gestured at Charles. "It just seems—''

"Never mind how it seems. I intend to marry Jordan and that's that.'' But if things were different and she had a choice between Jordan and Charles, who would she choose?

She put that thought out of her mind. There was no choice, so there was no use in even thinking about it.

"Uh, Mari?'' Kirby asked.

"Yes?"

"There's a phone call for you. I guess you were so, uh, involved, you didn't hear it."

"Okay, thanks, I'll take it in the kitchen."

Kirby shrugged and headed back to his lab, his unaccustomed foray into the vagaries of human nature apparently at an end.

She picked up the phone. "Hello?"

"Hello, dear, how are you?"

"I'm fine, Mom. What's going on?"

"I—we—your father and I—just wanted to apologize for the way we behaved at the dinner party." Her mother sounded oddly hesitant.

Mari sighed. "That's okay, Mom, I understand. The Sloans were unbelievably condescending."

"Yes, but that's no excuse. The dinner was important to you, and we just made it worse."

"It's okay, Mom," Mari repeated. The damage was done now.

"Dear, are you sure Jordan is...the right man for you?"

What was this, a conspiracy? "Yes, Mom, I'm sure."

"Well, then, I guess I need to tell you something," she said, an odd reluctance combined with resolution in her voice.

Do I really want to hear this? "Okay, tell me."

"Well, you know how your father always brags about being descended from Black Bart?"

She'd thought about nothing else for days. "Yes."

"Well, he's not really."

"I know—he's descended from his brother."

"No, I mean, he's not related to him at all. Well, he might be. We don't know. He's never researched the family tree that far back. But as far as he knows, he's not really related.''

"He's not?" Mari was incredulous. "Then why did he say he was?"

"Oh, you know how it is. People get to bragging and telling tall tales about their ancestors and your father just kind of followed right along. With the similarity in names, it was a natural assumption. It was fun and never hurt anyone...until now, that is.''

She could say that again. "Why didn't you tell me?"

"It didn't seem important, until your fiancé's parents gave you such a hard time about it."

Stunned, Mari didn't know how to answer. "I see. Well, thanks, Mom, for telling me."

"Do you forgive us, dear?"

"Of course. I—I just need to think about this a little. I'll talk to you later, all right?"

They said their goodbyes and Mari hung up, then just stood there trying to take it all in.

Charles entered the kitchen. "What's wrong?"

"That was my mother. She just told me we're not related to Black Bart after all. They just...made it up."

He regarded her gravely. "And how do you feel about that?"

"I don't know." Too many things had happened today. She was only conscious of an overwhelming feeling of frustration. Not only had her parents' fib jeopardized her engagement but she'd yanked Charles out of time and screwed up his life...for what? A relationship that didn't even exist?

"This is what you wanted, isn't it? To not be related to Black Bart?"

"Yes, but the timing stinks. I sure wish she'd told me this a couple of weeks ago—it would have saved a big mess."

"At least she's given you the means to clean it up."

Mari sat up straighter. "You're right." At least part of it could be fixed, anyway. "Let me call Jordan and tell him the good news."

She dialed and waited while the maid went to get him. "Jordan, hello. This is Mari."

"Hello. Did I miss something? Did we have a date?"

Did she call him so seldom that he had to ask this? "No, no. I just got off the phone from my mother and she had good news. I'm not related to Black Bart at all."

Silence, then, "You're not?"

"Right. Isn't it wonderful? They were just... kidding."

"Kidding? Some joke." Jordan's voice sounded forbidding. "I don't think my parents will find it amusing."

"But don't you see? Now your parents have no reason to object to me."

Silence again.

"Jordan?" Why was he so quiet?

"I...don't think this will help."

Exasperated, she asked, "Why not?"

"The damage is already done."

"But you can undo it with this information."

"No, I'm afraid my parents won't believe it. I'm not sure I believe it. It sounds too...convenient."

"How can you say that? I wouldn't lie."

"Oh, I'm not accusing you," Jordan assured her, "but your parents..."

"You're accusing my parents of lying?" she asked in an ominous tone.

He hesitated before replying. "Not lying, exactly, but...stretching the truth, maybe, to help their daughter."

"That's ridiculous. They wouldn't do that."

"Be reasonable. They either lied about being descended from Black Bart or they lied about not being related to him. Either way, they lied."

Put that way, she couldn't disagree, but Jordan made it sound so harsh. She chewed on her lower lip, not knowing what to say.

"Mari, dear?" Obviously feeling he'd won this round, Jordan's voice turned placating.

"Yes?"

"Why don't you let me take care of this? I'll tell my parents in my own good time."

"*Before* your birthday party?"

"I don't know. I'll wait until the time is right, okay?"

"Okay, I guess. But if you don't clear things up before then, they're not going to be very happy when you announce our engagement."

Silence again.

"Jordan? You *are* going to announce our engagement, aren't you?" She hated herself for letting her voice sound so pleading, but she couldn't help it.

"Of course, of course. Just leave everything to me."

"All right. I'll see you later—at the party."

Jordan said goodbye and she hung up, then turned to face Charles.

"I take it Jordan wasn't receptive?"

"You can say that again. He called my parents liars and said his parents wouldn't believe it. Now we're back where we started from."

"There's still the possibility I can find Black Bart and reform him myself—change all this before it even happens."

Mari considered it once again. "No, I don't think so."

"No?"

"No, I don't want you to. I've learned more about myself and how to deal with people these past few days than I have in my whole life. I wouldn't trade that for anything."

"Are you certain?"

"Yes. And this way I'll be able to remember you, too." This felt right—and it was more important to her than she'd realized.

Charles smiled at her and her heart turned over in her chest. His expression was so tender, so full of affection. Why couldn't Jordan look at her like that?

"I'm glad," he said. "I'd like to think of you remembering me."

"I just hope you'll be able to do the same."

He smiled. "Ah, I have a plan."

Her hopes rose. "What is it?"

"Kirby said he could send a note back with me, so I'm going to write about you."

"I don't understand."

"I've decided to put together a journal of our time together, everything I've experienced, all about you. That way, even if I don't remember, I'll have the journal to remind me."

Mari's eyes filled with tears. "Oh, Charles, that's so sweet."

He stroked her cheek and gazed into her eyes. "It's important to me. And when I get back to 1874 I'll continue writing in the journal for the rest of my life. I'll find some way to leave it to you, to make sure you get it after I die."

The tears were falling for real now. "Oh, Charles." She hated to think of him dying, years before she would even be born. "I do wish you could stay."

His fingers tightened in her hair. "So do I, Mari. You have no idea how much."

They stayed cuddled for a few moments longer, then Mari pulled away. "Well, it seems odd to have our goal of finding your memory suddenly gone. What do we do now? Do you want some time alone to write in your journal?"

"No, I'll do that later tonight. For now, and until I leave, I just want to fill the days with new experiences and create those beautiful memories you mentioned yesterday."

Mari choked back her tears. "All right, it's a deal. What would you like to do first?"

For the rest of that day and throughout the next two, they concentrated on giving Charles new experiences. Mari took him to the ethnic restaurants in town, to tantalize his palate with the distinctive flavors of Greek, Japanese, Mexican and French food, not to mention good, old American junk food like chocolate, ice cream, french fries and hot dogs.

Charles enjoyed them all and Mari found it fun just to watch him savor every morsel. In between meals they spent the time exploring the countryside and enjoying the beauties of nature so abundant in Sedona. In the evening Charles wrote in his journal.

Their enjoyment was marred only by the constant reminder of Charles's need to leave, punctuated by another of the vortex's insistent demands. It merely caused them to redouble their efforts to fill their days with activity. They visited the Chapel of the Holy Cross, built right into the mountain, explored the Montezuma Castle and Tuzigoot Sinagua Indian ruins and wandered the streets of the ghost town of Jerome.

On the morning of Jordan's birthday party Mari woke Charles and asked, "Are you ready for Oak Creek Canyon today?"

He smiled at her. "Of course. Whatever you say."

"Here," she said, tossing him one of Kirby's bathing suits. It had stretched out so much it ought to fit Charles. "Wear this under your jeans today."

Charles gave her a quizzical look, but nodded. Soon they were on their way in her Jeep.

"What's Oak Creek Canyon?" Charles asked.

"You'll see."

Driving down the highway through the canyon was a breathtaking experience, no matter what time of the year. The creek's clear, sparkling waters ran alongside the road, tumbling over large boulders and dappled by the shade of towering sycamores and cottonwoods.

Mari pulled over to the side of the road. "We're lucky. It's a weekday and school's in session, so there won't be many kids. We should have the place to ourselves."

She got out of the car and began pulling off her jeans. "Come on, take off your clothes. We're going in the water."

Charles regarded her with a puzzled look.

"It's okay—we both have bathing suits on."

He shrugged and did as she asked, then watched as she peeled down to her one-piece navy swimsuit. It was plain and unadorned, but Mari still enjoyed the look in Charles's eyes as he gazed at her appreciatively.

She couldn't help but return the favor, her gaze drawn inexorably to his broad chest, sprinkled with dark hair, and the strength of his lean body encased in the tight confines of Kirby's swimsuit. Mari inhaled on a breath of appreciation. He looked better than any man had a right to.

Before she embarrassed herself by staring too hard, she grabbed his hand and led the way down the embankment to the creek. "Come on, this'll be fun."

Perfect—there was no one here this time of the morning. They were alone with the chuckling stream and the gentle sighing of the wind in the trees.

Charles glanced around with a smile on his face. "This is beautiful."

"I thought you'd like it. But come here, I want to introduce you to the pleasures of Slide Rock."

"What's that?"

"It's a natural water slide. Oh, it's nothing like the water parks in Phoenix, but it's still fun—and a lot closer. Here, watch me and do what I do. Sit here and let the water take you down."

She entered the waist-high water, and with a squeal she was off, rushing down the length of the slide to be dumped into a shallow pool at the bottom.

She turned around to check on Charles and found him right behind her, his arms and legs spread out in delight. He gave a booming laugh as he spilled into the pool, almost swamping her with his entry.

He continued to chuckle as he stood, wiping the water from his face. "What marvelous fun. Can we do it again?"

"Of course, that's the idea."

They continued to ride the slide until Mari became tired. She waded to the edge of the pool and found a flat rock to sit on, dangling her legs in the water and watching the delight on Charles's face as he slid down the rock again.

But this time, instead of heading back up, he came to sit beside her. "Thank you," he said simply.

She grinned up at him. "For teaching you how to slide on a rock?"

"Yes, that, and for sharing all the other experiences with me. And...for being you."

The day was perfect—warm with just the hint of a breeze, and the heady glory of nature all around them. It was the only way Mari could account for what she did next.

Murmuring, "You're welcome," she leaned toward him and pressed her lips against his in a light kiss, her palm against his cheek.

He froze and stared at her, their lips only a kiss apart as their breath mingled. Boldly she repeated the kiss, letting her lips cling to his as she slipped her tongue into his mouth.

He tasted like freshness and sunshine...and forbidden pleasures. Charles embraced her, slanting his mouth against hers to deepen the kiss. Mari sighed and gave in to the moment, wanting it to go on forever.

Abruptly he broke off, clutching his stomach.

"What's wrong?"

"The...vortex," he gasped out. Beads of sweat appeared on his forehead and the veins on his neck appeared in stark relief as his face turned white with the strain.

Helpless, Mari could do nothing but watch as Charles writhed in agony before her. "Tell me what to do," she cried in anguish. She wanted to help, to take away his pain.

But Charles suffered in silence until his face suddenly relaxed and he slumped against her. "It's all right...it's over now."

"Oh, Charles," Mari said and hugged him tightly. She didn't want to let him go. Ever.

Chapter Thirteen

They'd been so busy helping Charles create happy memories that Mari hadn't had much of a chance to worry about the party tonight...until now. She should be elated. Tonight was the night Jordan was finally going to announce their engagement. It was the culmination of her dreams—the start of her new life.

And she had all the tools to make it a success. In her new burgundy-colored party dress, she looked better and more sophisticated than she ever had. And with Charles and Kirby's help, she had confidence she could survive tonight and probably even hold her own. So why wasn't she happier?

It was Charles, of course. If only Charles could stay here, her happiness would be complete. Mari sighed. She might as well wish for the stars. Kirby had confirmed he hadn't been able to come up with a way to help Charles stay without destroying Charles in the process—and that would sort of defeat the purpose.

She glanced at her bedside clock. Time to go. She gathered her purse and her wrap and went to the living room to find Charles and Kirby. Proud to be escorted by two such handsome men, Mari blinked back tears. Tonight was not the end, she reminded herself.

It was only the beginning—the beginning of her new life.

Touched by their support, she approached Kirby and smoothed an errant cowlick, straightened his glasses, then gave him a kiss on the cheek. "Thank you for coming tonight."

Kirby shrugged uncomfortably. She turned to Charles and kissed his cheek, saying, "Thank you, too. This means a lot to me."

Charles smiled and gave her an appreciative, seductive look that left her nerve endings tingling. "You're welcome, though I don't know why you need us this evening. You look absolutely lovely. I predict you'll be the belle of the ball."

"Yeah," Kirby added. "Beautiful."

Buster meowed at Mari's feet, in seeming agreement. "Thank you," she said again. "All three of you. Shall we go?" Jordan was unable to pick her up this evening. Since the party was in honor of his birthday, his mother had insisted he be there to greet his guests.

"Just one thing more," Charles said, and produced three small perfect rosebuds that exactly matched the color of her dress.

She smiled, touched. If he gave her flowers every other day like this, he was going to spoil her. She glanced down at her low-cut sweetheart neckline. "I—I don't quite know where to wear them."

Kirby gestured upward. "Why not in your hair?"

She gave him a surprised look. "Good idea. I'll just be a minute." She carefully placed the flowers in her upswept coiffure and smiled. It was the perfect touch to set off her ensemble.

Returning to the living room, she said, "Thanks,

both of you. Now I'm sure the evening will be perfect.''

They headed toward the car, though there was a little disagreement when Buster assumed he was coming along and Mari was just as adamant that he wasn't. They managed to make it out the door without him and enjoyed the drive to the Sloans' house.

When they reached the Sloans', Mari swallowed hard. This was it. The moment she'd been waiting for. Moths started dancing the rumba in her stomach, just like the other time she'd been here, and she wondered irreverently if the Sloans cultivated them for that purpose. She wouldn't put it past them to breed the species to discomfit uninvited guests.

Charles gave her a sympathetic glance, as if he knew about the aerial acrobatics going on in her insides. "Are you ready for this?"

Mari took a deep breath. "As ready as I'll ever be."

They entered the house, and after the maid took Mari's wrap and purse they waited in line to greet their hosts. Her heart sank when she received a cool nod from Reginald Sloan, then descended even further when his wife glanced at the flowers in Mari's hair and wrinkled her nose in distaste. Belatedly Mari remembered Myra was allergic to roses. Oh well, it couldn't be helped now.

Luckily Jordan's greeting made up for his parents' coldness. His eyes widened as he took in her appearance. "You look beautiful tonight, Mari."

Finally he noticed...but there was a possessive glint in his eyes she wasn't sure she cared for. "Thank you," she murmured. "Happy birthday. How long will you be in the receiving line?"

"Not much longer. Please, enjoy yourself. I'll catch up to you later."

Mari wanted to question him further, but Myra Sloan's annoyed glance showed she was holding up the line. Mari strolled off, Charles and Kirby right behind her. Not for the first time, she was very glad they were with her. If they hadn't been, she'd be wandering around looking lost right about now and probably tripping over one thing while spilling something else.

"Would you like something to drink?" Charles asked.

"I'm not sure I want to push my luck," she said. "I'll stay as far away from the food tables as possible."

"I'll get it for you," Charles offered.

It would help to have something in her hands, so she didn't feel so awkward. "Okay, but find something clear if you can, so it won't stain if I spill it."

Charles's answering glance was half amused, half reproachful. "You are *not* going to spill anything tonight. I won't allow it."

"Yes, sir. But you may not be able to stop it."

"You're going to do just fine. Wait here and I'll get you a drink."

He headed toward the refreshment table and Kirby followed him looking bewildered, as if he wondered what he was doing there.

As Mari waited, she glanced around. They had been steered into a large room, where all the furniture had been removed to allow for dancing and chairs were lined up around the wall. Mari eyed the chairs with a grimace. They reminded of her wallflower days.

The room was filling with handsome young men and a preponderance of highbred debutantes, whose every movement screamed class and sophistication. For once in her life Mari knew her dress was just right, giving her the confidence she needed to fit in.

A small trio of beauties approached Mari and introduced themselves as Babs, Tiffany and Trudy. Mari smiled, wondering what in heaven they wanted with her.

Babs turned out to be the spokesperson for the group. "We were watching you in the reception line. Do you know Jordan Sloan well?"

"Pretty well," Mari admitted.

"What's he like?"

When Mari hesitated, Babs said, "Just between us girls, we all know the Sloans invited a lot of women so he can take his pick. But we don't know anything about him. Do you?"

"Yes, but I hear he's already secretly engaged."

The faces of all three girls fell. "Too bad," Babs said. "It's not often looks, breeding *and* money all come together in one nice package." She gave Mari an arch smile. "And what about the other two? The men who came with you? The dark one is just divine."

Mari felt a stab of annoyance and her protective instincts leapt to the fore. "Charles? Oh, he's my cousin." Feeling wicked, she added, "He's sort of the black sheep of the family. Not at all the thing."

Babs cast him a wistful glance. "Oh. What has he done?"

"He—no, you don't want to know."

"Oh." Babs's disappointment was palpable, but she still continued. "What about the other one?"

Mari started to tell a similar story about Kirby, but hesitated. It would do him good to get some female attention for a change. Instead, she decided to tell the truth. "That's Kirby Jones," she said in a voice of great significance.

The interest in their eyes intensified. "Who's he?"

"You've never heard of him?"

The three glanced at each other and said in unison, "No."

"He's a genius. Works for a California think tank. They pay him oodles of money to work on problems no one has ever solved before."

"Is he married?" Babs asked.

"No."

"Engaged?"

"No. He doesn't even have a girlfriend."

"What about his family?" Trudy interjected.

Mari searched her mind, trying to remember what Kirby's father did now. Wasn't he a loan officer? "They're in banking," she explained.

The predatory gleam in their eyes grew stronger. Babs turned to look at him again with an assessing glance. "What's he working on now?"

Time travel sounded too far-fetched, so Mari searched her mind for a subject that would sound sexy enough to keep these three interested. She had it—the perfect clincher. She gestured for them to come closer and whispered, "Can you keep a secret?"

They nodded in unison.

"Well, don't tell anyone, but he's hot on the trail of...the secret to eternal youth."

Three pairs of plucked eyebrows shot up, followed by identical expressions of calculation and greed. As one, they turned to stare at Kirby who was headed their way, followed by Charles. "He is kind of cute," Babs said. "And he looks lonely. Maybe you could introduce us?"

Mari suppressed a smile. "Of course." When the men reached them, she introduced Kirby to the trio and pulled Charles away to leave them a clear field. Kirby just stood there with a bemused look on his face as the three pastel-clad vultures swooped down on him.

"What was that all about?" Charles asked.

"Oh, nothing. I just told them how eligible Kirby is, so they closed in for the kill." She didn't feel a bit of remorse. Kirby needed some attention, and she needed to protect Charles and Jordan. After all, Jordan was her fiancé and Charles was...what?

She paused. Why had she removed Charles from the running? Because he wasn't eligible, of course. How could he be considered eligible when he wasn't even going to be around next week?

He chuckled. "Closed in for the kill? That's an accurate description." He glanced around. "Where's Jordan? I thought he'd be here by now." He handed her a glass of clear bubbly liquid.

She took a sip, glad it was nothing stronger than soda. "No, he's still greeting guests."

"When is he going to announce your engagement?"

"I don't know—I assume sometime later, maybe when they sing 'Happy Birthday' to him."

Charles nodded. "Ah, I see him coming now."

Jordan strode up to Mari and Charles gave her a smile and a discreet thumbs-up, then faded into the crowd. Jordan ignored Charles, to smile down at Mari and take her arm possessively. "You look stunning. Come, let me introduce you around."

Jordan introduced her to the varied members of his social set, all of whom appeared to be beautiful, tanned and complete dilettantes. It seemed all they did was play and gossip.

Jordan thrived on the attention he was getting from his peers, especially the women, and as they progressed around the room his smile became wider and his possessiveness less pronounced. In fact, at times he seemed to even withdraw from her, as it became more apparent that he found her lack of social standing a liability.

As they left one group and headed for another, Mari groped for a way to speak to him alone. "Jordan, can we dance?"

He hesitated, but his manners were still intact. "Of course." He led her to the dance floor and she moved into his arms.

"Can I ask you a question?"

"Sure. What is it?" Though he spoke to her, his gaze darted around the room, as if he were looking to see who else he could impress.

"I'm confused. I thought you said you didn't fit in with these people." And now that she'd met them, she wasn't sure she wanted her fiancé to fit in with these pretty, useless social butterflies.

Jordan finally looked at her. "I never did before. I don't know what's changed, but isn't it wonderful? They like me now."

You mean they like your father's money, Mari wanted to say, but kept her mouth shut. And Jordan himself had come out of his self-imposed shell and was actively talking to people. Mari knew how a little self-confidence had helped her. It was obviously doing the same for Jordan. How could she complain? She wanted him to be happy, didn't she?

Yes, but she was afraid she'd lose him to these new friends of his before he realized how shallow they were. She glanced around the room. Charles was speaking with a few of the older guests and Kirby was surrounded by more of those pastel vultures, looking bewildered, flattered and harassed all at once. Seeing her friends nearby gave her the courage to ask the next question. "But Jordan..."

"Yes, dear?"

"When are you going to announce our engagement?"

"Our engagement?" He frowned, as if he'd only just now remembered it. "Uh, I haven't told my parents yet."

"You haven't? Oh, Jordan," she said in disappointment, "when are you planning on doing it? After we're married?"

"No, no, of course not. It's just that...the time hasn't been right."

"When is it going to be right?" she pressed. "You promised you'd announce it tonight."

He looked around at the sycophants who had hung on his every word and ran his finger around his collar. "Maybe...maybe we should think about this."

She couldn't believe she was losing him to these people. Was he so shallow he couldn't see the difference between these flatterers and real people like Charles and Kirby...and Mari? "Jordan, you promised. Are you going to break your word?"

His word was important to him, and Mari knew it. He nodded in resignation. "You're right. Let me just tell Mother, so it doesn't come as a complete shock.''

The dance ended and he led her to the side, then frowned and looked around. "I see Mother. Wait here and I'll tell her.''

Mari should insist she accompany him. After all, the announcement of an impending marriage ought to be a happy event, shared by all. But with Jordan describing the event as a ''shock,'' Mari had a feeling this wasn't going to be a pleasant experience.

Frustration filled her. This should be one of the happiest times of her life. Instead, she found herself worrying that Jordan would be distracted by his new friends and forget all about her—or Myra Sloan would keel over in a dead faint or refuse to countenance the marriage.

"Remember,'' Mari whispered to him. "I'm not related to Black Bart at all.''

Jordan nodded impatiently and left. Mari watched him go, with the sinking feeling this was not going to go well. But if Jordan would only remember to tell them she wasn't descended from Black Bart, all would be just fine. She just needed a chance—she was sure she could make his parents like her...in time.

Charles joined her then. "Is he going to make the announcement?''

"No. He's going to tell his mother.''

Charles didn't comment, just raised his eyebrows. "I see. Would you like to dan—'' His words broke off as he doubled over.

She grabbed his arm. "Charles, what's wrong?''

"Vor...tex,'' he gasped out.

People were starting to stare, so she pulled him into

one of the smaller rooms nearby. Luckily it was unoccupied, so Mari led him to the couch.

He sank down onto the cushion with a moan, his face contorted in pain.

She loosened his tie and unfastened a couple of shirt buttons, not knowing what else to do. "Charles, what can I do?"

"Nothing. I'll...be all...right."

Like hell he would. He was gasping for air. She searched the room frantically, hoping to find a glass of water—something that could help. Nothing there. She opened the door to a small adjoining room.

"Mari?" Charles called.

She abandoned her search and returned to his side. "Yes? What is it?"

"I'm all right now. It's stopped."

Mari gazed at him with compassion. "Oh, Charles, I'm so sorry. Was it very painful?"

"I'm afraid so. This one was quite severe."

"Worse than this morning?"

"Much worse. I'm afraid I don't have much time left. Soon I shall have to return to the vortex...and my own time."

Mari wanted to scream a denial, but she knew what he said was true. "But—"

"Shh," he said. "There's someone in the next room."

"That's Jordan," Mari whispered. "He must be speaking to his mother. I'd better close the door."

She started to rise, but Charles caught her arm. "No, they might hear you and think you're spying on them. Be silent and they'll never be the wiser."

He was right. She didn't want to be caught listening. How mortifying. She stilled, and the conversation floated into the room and their waiting ears.

"...to announce my engagement to Mari," Jordan said.

Elation rose within her. Finally!

"What?" Myra snapped. "That nobody? You can't do this to me...to your father."

"But, Mother, she's not really related to Black Bart. Her parents were only kidding about that—you have nothing to worry about there."

"Don't be silly," Myra said in an irritated tone. "We only used that as an excuse. Who cares about this Black Bart person? The fact is, she has no money and no background. She's not right for the son of Reginald Sloan and I won't have it, do you hear?"

Shocked, Mari could do no more than listen.

"But, Mother, I promised."

"Then unpromise. Dump her or pay her off. Do whatever you have to, but get rid of her. I refuse to be related to those wretched low-class parents of hers."

That was quite enough. It was bad enough that the witch slammed her, but when she lit into Mari's parents that was going too far. Seething with a rage like none she'd ever felt before, Mari rose to battle.

Striding to the open door between the two rooms, she halted to compose herself. Jordan stared at her in surprise and Mari spoke in the calmest tones she could manage while her heart thumped in her throat. "Speaking of low class, shouldn't you check to make sure you're not overheard before you broadcast slanderous remarks at the top of your lungs?"

"Mari," Jordan gasped. At least he had the grace

to look shamefaced, though she couldn't say the same for his mother.

"Yes, it's me. Your fiancée, or had you forgotten? The one you're supposed to love and *defend*?"

"Not yet, you're not," came Myra's rejoinder.

Mari had had it. "You're damn right I'm not. And I don't intend to be."

"What are you saying?" Jordan asked. His astonishment was mixed with a bit of hope, damn him.

"I'm saying I wouldn't have you if you were the last man on earth. You've changed, Jordan. You're no longer the sweet misfit you were when we first met. You've turned into a brownnosing egotistical jerk, a wimpy mama's boy—"

"How dare you," Myra exclaimed.

"Shut up," Mari snapped. "I'm not through. Jordan, you're so blinded by the flattery of your new friends that you can't see they're not interested in you—just your money."

"As if you weren't," Myra sneered.

Mari ignored her—it wasn't worth explaining. "And not only that, but *I* don't want to be related to *your* parents. They're nothing but a pair of windup dolls who are so dumb they think net worth equals self-worth. They wouldn't know a decent person if they walked up and shook their hands—they're too used to having their butts kissed."

Myra puffed up again, but Mari forestalled her impending tirade. "Oh, stuff it, Myra. You're getting what you want. I release your precious son from our engagement and will never speak to him again. I'm outta here."

Triumph gleamed in Myra's eyes. Mari expected that, but not the relief she saw in Jordan's. Blindly she turned to leave and found Charles there, supporting her.

She blinked back tears and Charles put an arm around her. "Are you all right?" he asked.

"Yes," she said, the adrenaline still flowing strong. "I'm great. Terrific. Get me out of here."

Charles nodded and steered her out of the room and into the ballroom, scooping Kirby up as they went along and extricating her belongings from the coatroom with finesse.

"What's going on?" Kirby asked with a puzzled look.

"Mari just terminated her engagement to Jordan," Charles explained.

Terminated—that was the right word. Mari the Terminator. She gave a humorless laugh. She'd just killed her last chance of belonging. It would hurt later. Right now, it just felt good to have told someone off for a change.

Kirby and Charles left her alone with her thoughts on the ride home, while Mari replayed the nasty scene in her head over and over again. Each time it got worse.

When they reached the house, she waited until they were all inside, then sighed and glanced up at Charles. "Guess I blew it, huh?"

He grinned. "I thought you were magnificent."

"You did?"

"Yes. I was cheering you on the whole way. Jordan's not good enough for you."

"That's right," Kirby said with feeling.

Mari turned to look at him in surprise and he reddened. "I never liked him," Kirby explained. "You belong with Charles."

"But Charles has to leave soon—" She broke off, suddenly remembering. "Oh, dear. In all the excitement, I forgot. Charles had another attack tonight."

Kirby shot him a concerned glance. "How bad was it?"

Mari answered for him. "Very bad—the next one may kill him, unless you can do something."

"All we can do is help him return to the vortex, return to his own time."

"No," she blurted out, an instinctive denial. She couldn't lose her dream *and* Charles. It just wasn't fair. Despite herself, she felt tears dampen her cheeks.

Kirby muttered something about checking the energy flows and left.

Charles gathered her in his arms and held her tightly. "Don't cry, Mari. It hurts to see you cry. Jordan isn't worth it."

Mari sniffled and clutched him tighter. "Don't you think I know that? That's not why I'm crying."

"Then why?"

She was crying over lost hopes, forgotten dreams, and soon, the loss of a cherished friend. "Because you're leaving and I'll never see you a-again," she said brokenly.

He led her to the couch and gathered her into his lap, stroking her back in comforting circles of warmth. "Mari, I want nothing more than to stay here with you forever—you know that."

"You do?" she asked in a quavering tone.

"Of course. You're the best thing that's ever happened to me."

"Yeah, in the whole week and a half of your memory."

He raised her chin to gaze into her eyes. "No, I

know deep within me that I've never known anyone like you, that I've never felt this way about anyone else in my life.''

Sheltered in the comfort of his arms, Mari gazed into his eyes and asked, "Felt what way?"

He gave her a tender smile and brushed a wisp of hair from her face. "As if you were the other half of my heart, my soul. As if we belong together throughout eternity, destined to find one another." He kissed her forehead. "As if you were my own true love."

"Love?" She somehow managed to get the word out, though her heart was beating like a wild thing. Did he mean...?

"Yes," Charles confirmed softly. "Don't you know by now that I love you with every fiber of my being?"

Her heart sang with pure joy. Charles loved her! Realization crashed in upon her. She had been so focused on belonging and finding a way to make Jordan keep his promise that she had overlooked Charles—his integrity, his whimsical sense of humor, his true friendship and his heavenly kisses.

No, she'd known it, but she hadn't let herself acknowledge it. She'd come to regard him with more than the affection of a dear friend. She realized now that she'd been fooling herself. No wonder she'd been so jealous of Charles at the party and was so devastated when she realized he had to leave so soon.

"Mari?" he asked tentatively.

"Oh, Charles," she cried, throwing her arms around his neck. "I've been such a fool. I love you, too."

"You do?"

She'd never seen pure joy on anyone's face until

now. Happily she nodded. "I do. Really I do." Her face crumpled into sadness as she held him tight. "But you must leave soon. What are we going to do?"

"There's nothing we can do," Charles said quietly. "But I can think of a pleasant way to pass the time..."

She hadn't realized you could feel sadness and joy at the same time. "So can I, Charles. So can I."

Chapter Fourteen

Charles's heart beat faster as he contemplated what Mari had said. "Are you certain?"

"Yes, I am," Mari answered with a tender smile and a caress of his cheek. "We have so little time left, and I don't want you to leave without making love to me first."

His heart swelled. She was offering a wonderful priceless gift—the gift of herself. "Even though it may be for only one night?"

"Yes, of course. At least this way I'll have a precious memory of you—one I can cherish and keep forever."

"That's quite a challenge you've set me," he said teasingly. "I wonder if I'm up to it."

She grinned and wiggled on his lap. "Oh, you're up to it. I can feel it."

Her squirming wasn't helping matters any. He caught her hips and held her fast. "If you don't want it to be over before it's begun, then you need to sit still."

She caught her lower lip between her teeth and gazed at him with contrition in her eyes. "I'm sorry."

"Ah, no, sweetheart. Don't be sad. It's my fault—

knowing you love me is pure intoxication, and the feel of you in my arms is so heady I can barely hold myself in check.''

"Really?"

He smiled at her continuing need for reassurance and swore to let her know then and there how much she affected him—especially in that flirty, sexy dress of hers. "Really. Let's take this slow and easy. I'm not sure when I shall have to go, but it probably won't be until sometime tomorrow. We have all night."

"All night," she repeated in an unsteady breath. "What...what shall we do?"

He smiled at her tenderly, understanding her real question. "Don't worry. You won't be clumsy at this. You couldn't be."

Mari blushed but still looked doubtful. Charles urged her off his lap, saying, "Come, let us find someplace more comfortable."

Shyly Mari led him toward her bedroom. He followed her into the darkened room. "Could you turn on the light?" he asked as he shed his jacket and tossed it on a nearby chair.

"The light?" she asked in a nervous tone.

"Yes. I want to see you, every inch of you, to memorize your beauty, your feel, your smell, your taste." This one night would have to last the rest of his life.

"All right," Mari said shyly. She chose a small bedside lamp and turned it on. Its dim light cast a golden glow about the room, chasing away the shadows and illuminating the room with a soft, romantic radiance. "Is this okay?"

"Perfect," he assured her, then loosened and removed his tie, discarding it on the chair as well. She stood trembling before him and he laid reassuring hands on her shoulders. "Are you afraid?"

She shrugged, then whispered, "Yes, I am."

"What are you afraid of? I won't hurt you."

"I know. It's just that…this is so important to me. I don't want anything to go wrong and I'm afraid I'll…I'll screw it up somehow."

"Do you love me?"

"Yes."

"Do you want to make love to me?"

"Oh, yes," she replied fervently.

"Then I can't think of a thing you could possibly do wrong."

She rolled her eyes. "Oh, *I* can. What about—"

He laid his fingers against her lips. "Shh. Everything will be fine. Just relax and let me do all the work." A sudden suspicion struck him. "This isn't your first time, is it?"

"No," she said in a small voice, her expression stricken. "Is that a problem?"

"Of course not. I just needed to know." She might not be a virgin, but she was as jumpy as one. Charles doubted her previous sexual encounters had been very satisfying, judging from her reaction.

Mari laughed nervously. "I'm sure it's not *your* first time, is it?"

Charles grinned. "I don't know. I can't remember." When she gazed at him in dawning understanding, he continued. "I can't remember anyone before you, so in a sense it will be my first time."

He could practically see confidence filling her until she beamed at him. "I hadn't thought about that."

"You will be gentle with me, won't you?"

Ah, just as he'd hoped, he surprised a chuckle from her. "Well, I'll try, but I can't promise anything."

"That's all I can ask." Unable to resist her any longer, he gathered her gently into his arms. For Mari's sake, he hoped he was experienced enough to do this right, to give her a night she'd never forget.

Gently he took the flowers from her hair and let the silky strands fall in glorious profusion around her shoulders. Burying his hands in her hair, he pressed his lips against hers and knew, suddenly, that he was going to have no problem at all. She trembled in his arms and he took his time, lavishing gentle kisses on her upturned face while he stroked the bare skin above her sinful dress. She moaned and wrapped her arms around him, opening her mouth to permit his tongue entry.

He probed gently, not wanting to startle her, wanting it to last. Her sweet uninhibited response sent his blood soaring and his body tingling. Resolutely he damped down the sensations as much as possible. If he gave in to his instincts, he feared he would have at her like a beast in rut.

She met his tongue stroke for stroke, then pushed him away. "I want to feel you against me," she murmured.

She gazed down at him, fumbling at the buttons on his shirt. He couldn't believe how arousing her innocent touch was. His excitement rose as her eagerness to see his body, touch him became apparent. He let her fumble with each button until they were all unfastened, then she tugged the shirt from his waistband and pulled it off his shoulders.

"There," she said with a sigh as she buried her fingers in his chest hair. "That's better."

She stroked his exposed flesh with eager fingers, her hands boldly exploring him. When they dropped to his waist and toyed with his belt buckle, he stopped her. "No, wait. Let me see you. I've been wanting to take this dress off you all night."

She pulled back nervously and Charles gave her a reassuring smile, letting his eyes speak of his love and desire for her. She caught her breath and stared at him as if she were mesmerized. He turned her around and slowly unzipped her dress, pressing a kiss on each exposed inch of her spine. When the zipper passed her waist, the dress no longer had any support, so it collapsed and fell in a heap at her feet.

She stepped out of it and he turned her to face his admiring gaze. Her strapless undergarment lifted her breasts, barely covering her nipples, taunting him with their nearness. He unfastened this barrier, too, and let it fall to the floor.

Awkwardly, Mari's arms came up to cover herself.

"No," he whispered. "Let me see." He pushed her arms aside and gazed intently at her upturned breasts with their dark, pouty nipples, taut with excitement. "You are so beautiful."

Without waiting for her reaction he took one of them in his mouth and suckled, while he filled his hand with the other. The contrast of her puckered nipple with the soft, smooth skin of her breast captivated him. He explored the contrasts with his tongue and fingers, stroking from smooth to hard, from hard to smooth, first concentrating on one, then the other.

Mari's breath came fast now and she cried out with small moans of pleasure, fueling his own increasing desire as she let him lavish his need on her breasts.

It wasn't enough. Abandoning her breasts for a moment, he kissed his way down her abdomen, to the lacy confection that covered her femininity. Caressing the soft cleft between her legs, he felt her heat and dampness through the soft silk. She gasped and he glided the material from her hips down her legs, until she stood totally bared before him.

The sight of her crisp brown curls, moist with desire, commanded his attention and made his own need that much more demanding. He buried his fingers in her sweet haven, intent on giving her pleasure.

She gasped aloud and drew back, reaching for his trousers. Wanting to be free of his constricting clothing, to feel her skin against his, Charles helped her remove his garments until there was nothing between them but anticipation.

She touched him then, a soft exploration of his genitals from rounded ache to yearning tip, then stroked the sensitive skin of his shaft with a firm hand. He gasped. It was too much. He stilled her hand, saying, "Wait."

He led her to the bed and lay down beside her. Returning his attention to her damp curls, he stroked her welcoming slickness until he found the small nub that would give her pleasure. As she made small whimpering sounds of delight, he bent to worship her breasts with his mouth and other hand, the hot, hard evidence of his desire pressed demandingly against the softness of her thigh.

As Mari's excitement rose, so did his, until he was hard put not to lose himself to mindless desire. Then, suddenly, she reached her peak and tumbled over it, gasping out his name and shuddering, pulsing with the strength of her exultation.

Ecstatic that he could give her such pleasure,

Charles gave in to the need so long denied him and rose to poise himself above her, his tip nudging her slick opening.

"I want you inside me," Mari whispered fiercely.

That was all he needed to know. With one movement he drove himself all the way inside her, and Mari gasped.

Suddenly contrite, he asked, "Did I hurt you?"

"No. Oh, no. Don't stop."

Relieved, Charles closed his eyes and filled his senses with the overpowering sensations of stroking in and out of his love, loving the way her legs wrapped around him and her inner muscles contracted to pull him in deeper, tighter.

So warm, so slick, so tight... He wanted it to last forever, but the need overtook him. He pumped harder, Mari meeting him stroke for stroke, until they appeared to be as one.

Her cries joined his as they rushed toward heaven, senses spinning and reeling out of control until he plunged over the edge of the abyss, into nirvana. He exploded with the sheer pleasure of it, then spiraled slowly back to earth and the reality of their entwined bodies.

Now totally sated, he slumped down next to Mari, and gathering her into his arms, he drifted off to sleep.

MARI WOKE AND GLANCED blearily at the bedside clock. Nine o'clock. So late? Her lips curved into a smile as she remembered why she had gotten so little sleep. They'd made love several times that night, each time a glorious celebration of their love, tainted only by the knowledge that these would be their last moments together.

She turned over to cuddle up to Charles, but he wasn't there. Instead, all she found was a single red rose. Smiling, she grabbed her robe and slipped it on to wander through the house, searching. They had so little time left, she wanted to spend every possible moment with him. She found him in the kitchen, fully dressed, his face creased in concentration as he put pen to paper, Buster draped in proprietary fashion over his lap.

"Hi," she said softly.

He glanced up and said, "Hi, yourself," his expression softening into lines of love.

She captured that expression in her mental picture gallery, trying to freeze frame this precious memory, complete with sight, sound and the incredible feeling of bittersweet love. She crossed the room to give him a lingering good-morning kiss. "What are you doing?"

"I've been writing my thoughts and feelings in the journal, while it's still fresh in my memory. Last night was so marvelous, so wonderful, I wanted to ensure I would never forget it." He set Buster on the floor and gathered her into his lap. "Mere words cannot encompass our transcendent experience, but I have to try. I don't want to forget you, Mari."

She nodded, blinking back tears. With a sudden surge of anger, she screamed soundlessly at the unfairness of it all. She'd finally found exactly where she belonged—in Charles's arms. Why did he have to leave?

"Mari? Are you all right?"

"I'm okay," she lied, her voice choking. "How long will it be?"

"I don't know—" He broke off, his face contorting as he doubled over, gasping for breath.

She slid out of his embrace. Dear Lord, what was happening to him? "Charles?" she said on a note of rising panic.

"Now," he gasped out. "It's now."

"No," she said. It couldn't be. She held his head in her hands. "Hold on. Maybe this one will pass, too." It had to—he couldn't leave her. She willed the pain away with all her might.

It didn't work. Charles still writhed in the chair. Helpless to know what to do, Mari was glad to see Kirby burst into the kitchen.

He glanced at Charles. "I just saw it on my monitor. It's happening now. We have to get to the vortex."

"No," she cried out. "Can't you stop it? Do something, Kirby."

"I can't," he said, his eyes full of pity. "We have to get him to the vortex *now*."

Really angry now, Mari said, "We have to do no such thing. If the vortex wants him, it can come and get him."

"It *is* coming to get him," Kirby said, his voice rising. "Can't you see that? For Charles's sake, we have to take him there ourselves."

"What do you mean?"

"The vortex is strong, but Charles has been resisting it so long I don't know what will happen if it takes him. If it jerks him back in time too hard, it might kill him."

"Why didn't you tell us this before?"

"Because I figured you two wanted to be together as long as possible. Besides, we can lessen the impact on him if we send him back using EVE *before* the vortex takes him.''

When Mari hesitated, Kirby pointed at Charles. "Look at him. Does it look like this is just a passing spell?''

Charles slumped against the table, clutching his stomach, white-faced with the agony he must be going through. "He's...right," Charles said. "Must... go.''

Suddenly convinced, Mari said. "Okay, but you're not going without me. Wait while I get dressed.''

She rushed into the bedroom and yanked on the first clothes she could find, then ran back out to the kitchen. From the window, she could see Kirby helping Charles into the Jeep, so she hurried out to join them.

Kirby strapped Charles into the back seat. "Hold on while I get EVE and my laptop.''

Mari went to sit beside Charles, but he shook his head. Grabbing her sleeve, he leaned close and said, "Journal. On the...table.''

The journal! Without that, he might not remember her at all. Mari hurried back inside and as she opened the door, a flash of gray and white sped past her. Damn—Buster was making another one of his escape attempts. Well, she'd just have to let him succeed this time. She had no time to mess with him.

Swiftly she grabbed the journal and returned to the Jeep. She helped Kirby strap down the machine, then scrambled into the seat.

Kirby sped out the driveway, heading toward the vortex, and Mari turned her attention to Charles. "How do you feel?''

"Not...so good," he said, clasping the journal to him as if it were a lifeline.

Kirby careened around another corner and a startled meow came from under the front seat. Kirby glanced down. "Buster. How'd he get here?"

"He sneaked out when I opened the door," Mari explained. "I didn't have time to catch him." Charles cut off a moan and she turned to look at him in concern.

He grimaced. "It's a little...better, closer to the...vortex."

"Good," Kirby shouted over his shoulder. "Maybe it will stop torturing you if it realizes we're coming."

"Wouldn't...count on it."

Mari choked back a sob. She'd never felt so helpless in her life. She wanted to take away his pain, destroy the vortex and its hold over him and keep him here with her—forever.

She prayed as she'd never prayed before in her life, rashly promising anything—*anything,* if only Charles could stay with her. He moaned in pain and she swiftly amended that. No, the most important thing was to keep him safe. *Please, God, don't let him die.*

Tears running down her face, she held Charles's hand tightly as Kirby sped toward the vortex.

"Don't...forget me," Charles whispered.

"I won't," she declared. "I'll love you forever."

"Love you...too."

She wiped away a tear and half sobbed, "Don't you forget me."

He patted the journal, still clasped in his arms. "I won't. I'll write...every day...leave it to...your ancestors...in my will...make sure you...get it."

"Oh, Charles." It was just like him to think of her. She sniffled and wiped the blinding moisture from her eyes. "Oh, God, I don't want you to go. Let me come with you."

"Can't."

Kirby risked a glance over his shoulder. "He's right. You can't go with him—I don't know how that would affect the fields. It might destroy you both."

She clutched Charles's hand even tighter. "Then I'll come to you—Kirby will find a way to get us together."

In the front, Kirby shook his head. "The same thing will happen to you that's happening to Charles now, but EVE won't be back in the past to help you. I won't risk it."

Her entire being shouting defiance, she yelled back, "It's my risk to take."

"No." Charles drew her hand to his lips and kissed it. The tension had eased from his face, as if the vortex really had lightened up on him. "Don't—I want to think of you...safe and sound. I...can't live unless you are. Promise me."

Stubbornly Mari kept her mouth shut.

"Promise me," he insisted. "I don't want to...worry about...you."

"All right," Mari conceded. "I promise. But if Kirby says it's safe, I'm going back—or I'll find a way to bring you here."

Charles nodded. "Fair enough." But she could tell from the look on his face that he didn't find it likely.

Kirby came to a screeching halt, slamming on the brakes. "We're here," he said unnecessarily.

He leapt out of the Jeep and ran to the back of it to fumble with his machine. There were a couple of cars parked alongside the road, and a man was going from car to car. When he reached them, he said, "Hey, man. You here for the vortex?"

"Yes," Kirby answered curtly.

"Well, it's not working right. You might want to try the one at Boynton Canyon—the energies at these two are all messed up."

"That's okay," Kirby told him as he lifted out his time travel apparatus. "We're going to fix it."

The man looked rather taken aback. "You are?"

"Yes," Mari snapped. "We caused it, so we'll correct it."

"But thanks for the warning," Kirby added. "Say, could you keep people away while we...do our thing? This might be dangerous."

"Sure," the do-gooder said and stepped away from the car. "Good luck."

"Thanks," Mari replied. "We'll need it." She helped Charles out of the car and half dragged him across the road. Panting, she said, "You're not going to make him climb Bell Rock, are you?"

"No," Kirby said, "we'll use the base around Courthouse Rock. That's how we brought him here, so that's how we'll send him home."

After he secured EVE on his back, he helped her support Charles. "Come on, let's go. There's no time to lose."

They hurried as fast as they could to the base of the rock and helped Charles find a comfortable place to sit. She sat there with him, cradling him in her arms and watched anxiously as Kirby set up his machine.

She tried to concentrate on mundane things, to avoid thinking of what was about to happen. "Don't forget," she called out, "you're going to set it so he can take his clothes back with him—and the journal."

"Right," Kirby said. "I've got it. Move away from him."

She glanced down at Charles. Let him go? "Do I have to?"

"Yes," Kirby insisted, "or you'll go, too. And that might be fatal—for all of us."

She glanced down at Charles and found him gazing at her with love in his eyes. "I love you," he whispered. "I'll love you until the end of time."

Unable to say much past the tears choking her, Mari said, "Me, too." It was inadequate to express the all-encompassing love she felt, but it would have to do.

Besides, after the previous night, she was sure Charles knew how she felt. But just in case, she poured all her love, her pain, her hope into one scorching kiss…their last. Cupping his cheek in her hand, she whispered, "Take care."

"I will," he whispered back. "You, too."

"Mari," Kirby said, "you have to move. Now."

Reluctantly Mari let go of Charles and stepped back, letting her fingers linger in his as long as possible until distance forced them apart.

She heard the hum of the machine and saw its distinctive violet glow. She backed away farther, her hand covering her mouth to muffle her sobs as Kirby turned up the gain.

"Any moment now," Kirby called out.

Charles watched her with eyes full of sadness and regret as his slumped form seemed to sparkle with a thousand points of light.

Suddenly a gray-and-white form streaked past

Kirby, heading for Mari. Buster! In horror, Mari realized the cat would pass right through the field. "No!" she cried, her hand outstretched in warning.

Too late. Charles and Buster had both disappeared.

Chapter Fifteen

Mari's grief at Charles's departure was overshadowed by dread. "Kirby, what happened? Is—is Charles going to be okay? And Buster?"

Kirby peered at the small screen of his laptop computer. "I don't know. The energy flows should be calming down, but they're as strong as ever. With Buster in there..."

He trailed off as icy horror seized her in its grip. Had Buster's untimely arrival destroyed them both?

Kirby, who looked as troubled as she felt, fiddled with his machine and the computer. "Wait, there's something happening."

Mari could feel the air crackle, then all of a sudden Buster reappeared with a small boom and explosion of dirt. He hung suspended in the air for a timeless instant, all four paws and tail fully extended with his short hair fluffed out to its maximum length.

Then the field let go and he fell to earth with a surprised "Yeow!" and laid there, apparently half stunned.

Mari rushed to pick him up and Kirby yelled, "Grab him and get out of the way, both of you. Something else is happening."

She snatched Buster off the ground and retreated to where Kirby was standing. She soothed the poor kitten, though he didn't seem to be too much the worse for his experience.

"Why did Buster come back?" she asked.

"Time probably expelled him, sent him back here because this is where he belongs."

"Oh." She'd hoped...but Charles didn't belong in this time.

She glanced at Kirby and noticed his eyes widen as he stared at the computer screen. "What's wrong?" she asked.

"There's—"

An explosion rocked them, throwing them off their feet. Mari curled into a ball to protect Buster, then shielded her head as fist-sized red rocks rained down on them. None of them caused much damage, but she could tell she'd have bruises tomorrow.

When the hail of rocks stopped, she glanced at Kirby. "Are you okay?"

"Fine, but I can't say the same about EVE."

She glanced at EVE. He was right—most of the rocks seemed to have picked that point to fall on and the machine was dented, its delicate components smashed.

Kirby pulled his computer out from underneath his body. "But at least I saved my laptop."

"What caused the explosion?"

A moan came from close by, and Mari jerked her head around to see a body half buried beneath the rubble.

"I think *he* did," Kirby said unnecessarily.

Mari's heart leapt in wild hope. "Charles?"

She and Kirby hurried across the rubble and she

shoved rocks out of her way as fast as possible. The man's head rose so she could see his face.

Elation surged through her and she yelled "Charles!" then threw herself at him, hugging him as hard as she could.

He grinned weakly. "I'm not Charles."

She leaned back to regard him in concern. "Have you lost your memory again?" She scanned the rubble around him. "Where's your journal?"

"No, Mari, I haven't lost my memory, I regained it. I'm not Charles Boles, I'm Benjamin Pierce."

Relief flooded through her. "I don't care who you are, I'm just glad you're back...Benjamin." She gave him a long, deep, satisfying kiss, then chuckled. "So that's why that name popped into your head so easily when you invented a fictional admirer for me."

"Yes, but I don't feel like a Benjamin anymore. You've made me into a Charles." He turned to give Kirby a wry look. "And I'm not from the past, I'm from the future."

"The future?" Mari repeated dumbly.

Kirby smacked his forehead. "Of course. I was right the first time." He turned to Mari. Remember we tried the vortex at Bell Rock first because I thought it went to the past?"

"Yes."

"Well, it *did* go to the past. I just didn't realize it because we didn't find anyone at Funk Hill in 1874."

Realization dawned. "Because my parents gave me the wrong date—a year off."

"Right. So when we switched vortexes, instead of going a hundred and twenty-three years into the past, we went a hundred and twenty-three years into the future."

Mari regarded Charles in amazement. "So you're from..."

"2120," he supplied.

Several things became clear all at once. "That's why you expected the bedroom door and the car door to open for you?"

"Yes. And also why Kirby's hypnosis didn't work."

"Of course it didn't," Kirby said. "I made the basic assumption—incorrectly—that you were from the past. No wonder you couldn't remember anything from 1874."

Mari wrinkled her brow. "But I'm confused. You knew so much about that time period and you spoke as if you belonged there. How could that be?"

Charles grinned. "That part's easy. You see, I'm an historian who specializes in the old west, specifically stagecoach robbers. When Kirby's machine grabbed me, I was on Funk Hill for research purposes. And I had so immersed myself in the writings of the time that the ebb and flow of the language came naturally to me when you said I was from 1874."

Their chitchat was fascinating, but she'd avoided the big question long enough. "How...how long can you stay this time?"

They both turned to look at Kirby. He glanced at the laptop, still clutched in his hands and said, "As far as I can tell, forever. The energy flows have returned to normal."

Elation rose within her. "You mean...Time is no longer out to get him?"

"Apparently not."

"But why did it give up so easily?"

Kirby gestured at the kitten, who had joined their

small group and was curled up on Charles's chest purring madly. "Perhaps Buster's presence threw a monkey wrench into the works, confusing Time enough so it sent both of them back by mistake."

"Maybe," Charles said. "But I have a different theory. This experience jarred loose all my memories so I remember everything—including my first trip through time. That time, it seemed as if I traveled down an endless tunnel of light, with images and ideas assaulting my brain from all sides. I thought I was dead."

With that kind of stress, it was no wonder he'd lost his memory. "But this time?"

"This time, I felt the push of the time machine and the pull back to my own time...but I think there was another force present, one pulling me back to now. I only went a short distance into the future, then the backlash snapped me back to the present."

"And probably caused the explosion," Kirby mused.

"Right."

"But what was that force?" Mari asked.

Charles smiled at her. "Haven't you guessed? It was the power of our love."

Mari stared at him in awe. It was that strong? As realization dawned, she grabbed Charles in a bone-crushing hug. "You can stay," she whispered in relief. Then a thought struck her and she hesitated. "Do you still want to? Now that you know who and what you are?"

He kissed her lingeringly. "Of course. Benjamin Pierce is a dried-up stick of a man, with no living relatives and few friends, whose idea of a good time is reading dusty, old history books. I much prefer the way you've helped me reinvent myself. I'd rather be Charles Pierce, here with you."

Mari's heart was so full, she could do nothing but tighten her arms around him.

Charles grinned. "You know what this means, don't you?"

"No, what?"

"You're going to have to marry me."

Her heart almost bursting with joy, Mari said, "Of course I'll marry you...but why do you say I have to?"

"Because Charles and Mari Pierce built a monument at the crest of Funk Hill."

"We did?"

"We *will*—and that's what drew me to that location in the future. It's a monument to the most famous stagecoach robber of all time—Black Bart, the reluctant rogue who brought us together across time."

COMING NEXT MONTH

#697 SPUR-OF-THE-MOMENT MARRIAGE by Cathy Gillen Thacker
Wild West Weddings
Cowboy counselor Cisco Kidd never expected to be a fifteen-minute fiancé in a client's matchmaking plans. His intended, Gillian Taylor, was certainly anxious to say "I do." While her sexy sass turned on his every desire, her eyes held secrets—secrets he'd spend their required honeymoon seducing from her.

#698 PLEASE SAY "I DO" by Karen Toller Whittenburg
Three Weddings & a Hurricane
Rik Austin wouldn't let wedding planner Hallie Bernhardt disrupt his plans to disrupt this wedding. He knew just what to do—a little tequila here, a little seduction there. Before she knew it, Hallie would be bewitched and bewildered—and the wedding would be history. But a funny thing happened on the way to disaster....

#699 VERDICT: PARENTHOOD by Jule McBride
Big Apple Babies
Overnight, the "Sexiest Man in Manhattan," Grantham Hale, became the adoptive daddy of quadruplets *and* twins! But his real troubles start when the quads' presumed-dead—but very much alive—biological mother reappears and the judge sentences Phoebe and Grantham to be parents... together!

#700 MR. WRONG! by Mary Anne Wilson
Guardian angel Angelina had worked hard to turn Melanie Clark into the proper mate for "Mr. Perfect." But *now* Angelina finds out Melanie is destined for Mr. Perfect's rougher, tougher, untamed brother...a guy Melanie can recognize at forty paces as Mr. Wrong!

AVAILABLE THIS MONTH:

Look us up on-line at: http://www.romance.net

HARLEQUIN WOMEN KNOW ROMANCE WHEN THEY SEE IT.

And they'll see it on **ROMANCE CLASSICS**, the new 24-hour TV channel devoted to romantic movies and original programs like the special **Romantically Speaking-Harlequin® Goes Prime Time.**

Romantically Speaking-Harlequin® Goes Prime Time introduces you to many of your favorite romance authors in a program developed exclusively for Harlequin® readers.

Watch for **Romantically Speaking-Harlequin® Goes Prime Time** beginning in the summer of 1997.

If you're not receiving ROMANCE CLASSICS, call your local cable operator or satellite provider and ask for it today!

Escape to the network of your dreams.

Let's Celebrate!

LOVE & LAUGHTER™

invites you to the party of the season!

Grab your popcorn and be prepared to laugh as we celebrate with **LOVE & LAUGHTER**.

Harlequin's newest series is going Hollywood!

Let us make you laugh with three months of terrific books, authors and romance, plus a chance to win a FREE 15-copy video collection of the best romantic comedies ever made.

For more details look in the back pages of any Love & Laughter title, from July to September, at your favorite retail outlet.

Don't forget the popcorn!

Available wherever
Harlequin books are sold.

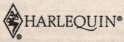 HARLEQUIN®

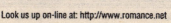